D0826881

NO WEDDING LIKE NANTUCKET

A SWEET ISLAND INN NOVEL (BOOK THREE)

GRACE PALMER

Copyright © 2020 by Grace Palmer

All rights reserved.

No part of this book may be reproduced in any form or by any electronic or mechanical means, including information storage and retrieval systems, without written permission from the author, except for the use of brief quotations in a book review.

❀ Created with Vellum

JOIN MY MAILING LIST!

Click the link below to join my mailing list and receive updates, freebies, release announcements, and more!

JOIN HERE:

https://readerlinks.com/l/1060002

ALSO BY GRACE PALMER

Sweet Island Inn

No Home Like Nantucket (Book 1)

No Beach Like Nantucket (Book 2)

No Wedding Like Nantucket (Book 3)

No Love Like Nantucket (Book 4)

Willow Beach Inn

Just South of Paradise (Book 1)

Just South of Perfect (Book 2)

Just South of Sunrise (Book 3)

NO WEDDING LIKE NANTUCKET

The wedding of the year versus the storm of the century. Who will win?

Things are finally looking up for the Benson family.

After a year of tough choices and big leaps of faith, it seems like love, success, and happiness are right in their grasp.

But with a wedding on the horizon and a successful new restaurant growing faster than anyone ever expected, everyone certainly has their hands full.

In fact, it's starting to cause problems.

Little cracks are appearing in the surface.

And the historic storm brewing offshore might turn those cracks into craters.

Can the Bensons and their loved ones band together in time to make this summer their best yet?

Or will jealousy and uncertainty spoil the big day?

Find out in NO WEDDING LIKE NANTUCKET.

Welcome back to another summer at Nantucket's Sweet Island Inn! It's the happiest time of the year, so sit down, stay awhile, and fall in love in this heartwarming, inspirational women's fiction beach read from author Grace Palmer.

PART I

ONE YEAR LATER

1

MAE

A beautiful Sunday morning in June.
Seven days until Eliza's wedding.

∼

These days, Mae Benson sometimes—not very often, but sometimes —slept in.

It was only on days when there were no guests at the Sweet Island Inn and no pressing chores to do. Only on days when she didn't have plans to meet a friend for brunch or volunteer at the pet shelter or the soup kitchen. Or if she'd stayed up late drinking a glass or two of wine on the front porch the night before.

So, not very often. But sometimes. And that alone was a world of difference from what she'd done for the first sixty-two years of her life.

As she entered year number sixty-three, a lot of things were different. Mae was now the permanent co-owner and co-operator of the Sweet Island Inn, a beloved bed and breakfast on the beautiful island of

Nantucket just off the coast of Cape Cod. She was a grandmother three times over. And she was beginning a new relationship.

"Beginning" was a heck of a word, though. As was "relationship." And "boyfriend," and "date," and "love," and all the myriad things that went along with falling for someone new at such an unexpected stage in her life. Just a few years ago, Mae would have thought that all those things had long since disappeared in the rear-view mirror. Oh, how wrong she had been!

Life came in circles, as it turned out. Seasons. And this was a beautiful springtime in her world, the kind where all the flower buds were just pushing their way up out of the topsoil. Things in Mae's universe were tender, blooming, and determined to reach the sunlight.

Speaking of sunlight, the rays coming through the blinds in the inn's master bedroom were letting her know that she had slept in plenty long enough. She rubbed the sleep from her eyes as she sat up and looked to her left. Her boyfriend, partner in crime, and fellow co-owner of the Sweet Island Inn, famed Irish novelist Dominic O'Kelley, was fast asleep next to her. Even unconscious, he looked the same as he always did—dapper, intelligent, reserved, with a soft smile playing across his lips.

She decided to be kind and let him sleep in for a little while longer. He'd been up late last night writing the first pages of his new novel. Staying as quiet as she could, Mae slipped out of the bedroom.

There were no guests at the inn today, nor would there be any for the rest of the week. It was closed for a special occasion: the wedding of Mae's oldest daughter, Eliza. Seven days from now, her firstborn would be standing on the altar, across from a man who had stolen her heart when she'd thought it was irretrievably broken. Just the thought of that moment made Mae smile.

With no guests requiring her attention, there was only herself and Dominic to take care of. Downstairs in the kitchen, she put on a kettle to heat water for the French press and found a yogurt in the fridge to quell the hunger in her belly. Though it was all well and good that there were no guests, Mae did miss having them. She loved how far people traveled to stay under her roof and explore the island she called home. She considered it a privilege to be able to host them. It was a responsibility she took quite seriously—"her life's calling," she said whenever anyone asked. After all, Nantucket was beautiful. Paradise on earth. In her humble opinion, everyone ought to see it at some point in their lifetime.

When the kettle began to squeal, Mae poured it over the coffee grounds and set a timer to let the coffee steep. She looked around, twiddling her thumbs. It was so oddly silent with no one here. No squeaks from the floorboards upstairs, no children running underfoot. The only thing that moved were the leaves of a rosebush outside the kitchen window, stirred by the early June breeze.

It still made her head spin to think about how fast this inn had become home. Two years ago, she had been living a different life. Then she'd lost her husband, Henry, to a tragic boating accident. In the wake of his death, Mae had taken up her sister-in-law's offer to manage the Sweet Island Inn in her absence. Mae had made the transition here from the house on Howard Street, the one she'd raised her family in, the one that Henry had built with his bare hands. That was an abrupt change. But it felt like the inn was her home from the second her bags first hit the ground. Funny how that worked—how home could travel with a person, change shape and size and smell, but still feel much the same every time you walked in the door.

Dominic joked sometimes that she was like a hermit crab. She'd shed one home—albeit not quite by choice—and picked up another. The old home felt somehow foreign to her now, despite how many of her memories and how much of her DNA was bound up in its walls. So foreign, in fact, that she'd recently begun the process of selling it. That thought—getting rid of the house on Howard Street—would once have seemed laughable.

But it wasn't. Not anymore. The Sweet Island Inn was home now. The house on Howard Street was merely a building she once had loved.

Everything she loved now was here with her. This inn, its spirit, its guests, her boyfriend, the island of Nantucket as a whole.

"Good morning, Sleeping Beauty!" she chirped brightly as the boyfriend in question made his way sleepily downstairs. Dominic was wearing a muted gray cardigan and olive green slacks with house slippers on his feet. Mae loved teasing him about the slippers. "Such an old man affectation," she'd say.

"As befits an old man," was his inevitable grinning reply.

He crossed from the bottom of the stairs to the kitchen, then let his fingers tap dance gently across the back of Mae's hand where it rested on the kitchen countertop. "What mischief are we getting into today?"

"Mischief? You've got the wrong girl for that," Mae answered. "I'm far too old for mischief."

"That's where you're wrong, darling. Mischief is merely a state of mind."

"The state of *your* mind, maybe. My mind is in a state of hunger right now. Yogurt isn't quite going to do it today."

"Well then, you're in luck, Mae, my dear. Sit back, sip your coffee, and prepare to be amazed." He cracked his knuckles and his neck, still grinning all the while.

"Uh-oh," she tutted. "Don't tell me you're going to cook."

"Not only am I going to cook," he said, walking over to the refrigerator and rummaging around, "I'm going to cook you the world-famous Dominic O'Kelley Toast Extraordinaire."

Mae wrinkled her nose. She was trying to bite back her laugh—Lord knows Dominic didn't need the encouragement when he got going like this, with such pep in his step—but she wasn't doing such a good job of keeping her smile hidden from him.

"What makes it so extraordinary?" she asked.

"That is a secret I'll take to my grave," he answered. "Now, shoo. I'm annexing this kitchen into my domain."

She laughed, shook her head, and went to fetch the newspaper from the stoop outside. It had been two years since Dominic first walked into her life. Two years of listening to that rolling Irish brogue, and yet she never tired of hearing how words came out of his lips, smooth like mossy pebbles in a riverbed. *Toast* wasn't just crisped-up bread when Dominic said it. It was something new, something special, something different.

But he was a terrible cook, so her expectations for the dish itself were quite low. She'd probably just have another yogurt when he wasn't looking. What he didn't know wouldn't kill him, right?

She chuckled under her breath as she opened the front door and stepped outside into the Nantucket June sun. It wasn't yet hot, but it would be, no doubt. The sun was making its way up the sky like an egg yolk sliding around in the pan. Clear blue sky, not a cloud in sight, and the not-so-distant murmur of waves sliding across the sand. Marvelous.

She eyed the mailbox at the end of the drive and had a quick internal debate about whether she ought to drag her tail down there to see if they'd received anything. She decided that if the bird feeder on the side of the house was empty, it was a sign she should go fetch the mail. Sticking her head around the doorjamb, she saw that it was in fact empty.

"Drat!" she said to herself, laughing. Oh well. A little stretch of the legs on such a fine day wasn't exactly cruel and unusual punishment. She had a sneaking suspicion that one of the squirrels who lived in the pine tree in the neighbor's yard was responsible for emptying the bird feeder. Dominic, whose little writing nook upstairs looked out on the tree in question, had named the squirrels. He swore he could tell them all apart, but Mae was doubtful. Pistachio, Cashew, Pecan, Almond, and Walnut looked way too similar for that.

She kept an eye on the tree, looking for any Nuts who looked particularly well-fed, as she waltzed down to the mailbox. When she got there, she saw that it was bursting full. "Oh goodness." Dominic's publisher must have forwarded all his fan mail here. They got bundles of the stuff periodically. It always fell to Mae to force Dominic into a seat so he could respond to the letters. Left to his own devices, Dominic would've used them for wall insulation. *Typical man*, she bemoaned. *No sense of personal touch whatsoever.*

She hefted the bundle under one arm, newspaper under the other, and made her way back inside. The squirrels must be sleeping off their illicit snack. Lucky little critters. They'd catch her wrath if she saw them stealing from her feeder again.

She coughed as soon as she crossed the threshold back into the living room, finding it filled with acrid smoke. The fire alarm was going off, too. She waved a hand in front of her face, still coughing, and ran into the kitchen. Dominic was standing in the middle, flapping a dish towel frantically at the toaster, where all the smoke was coming from. When he saw that she'd returned, he froze and looked at her like a little kid caught doing something naughty.

"'World famous,' my behind!" She laughed. "Get out of my kitchen, you goon, before you burn the whole house down." She took the dish towel from his hand and swatted him on the bottom as he trudged sheepishly past her.

Typical man, she thought again. But he was *her* typical man.

That was marvelous, too.

2

ELIZA

No one had ever told Eliza Benson that wedding planning was so freaking difficult.

Actually, that wasn't true. Lots of people had told her. Just like lots of people had told her that motherhood was hard. She hadn't listened to that, either. Wrong on both counts, as it turned out. Wedding planning was hard. Motherhood was hard. She really ought to start heeding others' warnings.

Lord, was she getting stubborn as she approached her mid-thirties! She was becoming more like her sister Sara. And, now that she thought about it, Sara was becoming more like her, too. Like a strange, Freaky Friday-esque switching of bodies and personalities. Sara the business owner? Eliza the headstrong? That was completely backwards.

And yet, it was the state of the world these days. Such is life, she had learned. *We grow, we change, we all turn into our parents.* It was both a blessing and a curse.

Speaking of parents, Mom was thriving these days. It made Eliza's heart sing to see her so happy with Dominic. It was still weird, of course, to see her mother in the arms of a man who wasn't her father. But Dominic was a good man; he loved Mom and he treated her well.

Happiness was by no means limited to Nantucket's Sweet Island Inn, either. Eliza's house was full of joy, full of her daughter's laughter and her fiancé's music.

After their spontaneous, preemptive, quasi-but-not-quite-honeymoon to Bermuda, the burgeoning Patterson family had come home to Nantucket. They were tan and in love with each other. Eliza loved Oliver, Oliver loved Winter, Winter loved Eliza. Winter, coming up on eighteen months, loved lots of things. She loved clapping and the song "Wheels on the Bus" and waddling around the house at breakneck speed. She had a little toy guitar that she played while Oliver made up words to songs, and when he picked her up and raced down the hallway with her, Winter squealed with that little girl laughter that instantly melted Eliza's heart.

As a matter of fact, that was what they were doing right this second. Oliver called the game "Rocket Ship." He made the sound effects to match as he zoomed up and down the hallway in his socks, sliding across the hardwood with Winter held out in front of him so she could feel the wind on her face.

"You know, some of us are trying to work!" Eliza hollered after him with a smile on her face. She was seated at the computer that lived in one corner of the living room, working out the kinks of a new set of Facebook ads for the Sweet Island Inn. Since Dominic's purchase of the inn from Aunt Toni, Eliza had been officially installed as the inn's business manager. Dominic had even ordered her business cards, which was both thoughtful and completely unnecessary. Honestly, the inn did all the work for her. Who could resist the allure of Nantucket in the sunshine? Beaches and lighthouses and quaint shops lining the cobblestone streets—*sign me up, please,* was the standard response. Eliza checked on the set of ads she'd pushed through this morning. There were already a few comments from potential customers.

OMG—how do i get here?? said one.

Heaven on earth, said another.

Eliza grinned. Well, they weren't wrong.

"Work, shmork!" Oliver shouted back as he *vroom-vroom-vroomed* back down towards Eliza. Winter was still cackling like a maniac.

"You better make sure she breathes," Eliza warned. "I can see all the blood rushing to her face already."

"This is literally the greatest moment of her life thus far," Oliver shot back as he got a running start and went skidding down the hallway once more. "Until tomorrow's session of Rocket Ship, that is."

She could only laugh and shake her head. She might be getting more stubborn these days, but she was no match for her fiancé. Oliver did what Oliver wanted, no matter the time or place. Luckily for her, what he usually wanted was to treat her like a queen and make her laugh. Sure, he got on Eliza's nerves every now and then, but what kind of couple lived a perfect life around the clock? She was far from perfect, and so was he. But their cracks lined up nicely.

A ding on the computer drew her attention as Oliver and Winter collapsed onto the living room carpet, giggling. Winter immediately crawled over to the toy bucket in the corner. She picked up her favorite toy—an oversized purple bubble wand—and handed it to Oliver. "Bub-bub!" she cajoled, clapping her hands. "Bub-bub!"

Oh goodness. As if Eliza's heart hadn't melted enough already. She and Oliver might not be perfect, but Winter was an angel sent from the heavens above. Well, most of the time.

She watched as Oliver pretended to consider Winter's request. He was going to give in, of course—duh; he was a softie for their little girl —but they both held back laughter as Winter's eyes got big. She tugged on his wrist and said it again and again—"Bub-bub! Bub-bub!"—until he cracked a huge smile, unscrewed the wand, and started to fill the living room with huge, iridescent bubbles that drifted around in the lazy draft of the fan overhead. Winter stood stock-still in the middle of it all, reaching out one chubby little finger in wonderment. Every time a bubble popped near her, she jumped a little in surprise and giggled.

Another ding on the computer drew Eliza's attention. Turning back to the monitor, she saw that an email had come in. Oliver must've left his email account open. "Babe, you got an email," she called over.

"Check it for me." He looked occupied with trying to top his personal record for how many bubbles he could get going at once.

Shrugging, Eliza double-clicked the notification and pulled his email up. She read it, blinked, read it again. "That can't be right ..." she mumbled under her breath.

"Everything okay?" Oliver asked.

"Uh, yeah, all good," she said. "It's, uh ... just check later when you have time."

"Sure thing, babe." Scooping up Winter, he went to scrounge up some snacks in the pantry.

Eliza sagged back in the chair, brow furrowed. It wasn't like Oliver to keep secrets from her, but it seemed like she'd accidentally stumbled across just that. The email that had come in was from a job recruiting site. It said, "Your application has been accepted—please select an interview time below."

Oliver was looking for a job?

That was news to Eliza.

It had been an ongoing topic over the last year. An understandably confusing one. After everything that had happened during their short stint on the Fever Dreams tour the previous summer, Oliver's music career had taken a strange and unexpected twist. He'd done well while he was performing. Better than he'd ever expected. That didn't surprise her. Everyone who had ever heard him sing and play the piano, even back in those days when he was just playing for tips at Nantucket bars, knew he was talented. But there's a difference between "talented" and "making it big." And it was awfully hard to say which side of that line Oliver fell on. The difference came down to luck. The guys who made it weren't always better than the guys who didn't. They just happened to be in the right place at the right time.

The question was whether Oliver could keep waiting until he made it. Sooner or later, his lucky break would come. He knew that; she knew that. But what if it didn't come until a *lot* later? He had a family now—a fiancée and a little girl. They wanted to build a life together. He couldn't be in two places at once.

He had to choose.

And last year, it seemed like he had chosen *them*. He'd wavered, sure. He and Eliza had rehashed that plenty in the days and weeks since then. But every time they talked about it, he answered with firm resolve: he chose them. He chose his family. He chose his girls. He might not get fame, but he'd always be able to have them. Night after night, day after day, he reiterated that decision with every kiss, every wink, every game of Rocket Ship.

That, Eliza was learning, was real love. Waking up each morning and choosing your partner again. That was the hard part, the work of it all. Not a single day could pass without making that choice.

It wasn't easy. Eliza knew that the cost of his choice still weighed on him, no matter how strong his conviction. He loved Eliza and Winter, yes, but he'd loved music first. He'd loved music since he was a little boy looking for somewhere to belong, and he'd wandered into the music room after school. Eliza adored that story. Every time Oliver told it, she closed her eyes and pictured a miniature Oliver—hair flopping over his face, shrunk down to four foot nothing, but with those green eyes shining exactly the same as they did now—stepping up warily to a piano, pressing a single key and hearing it ring out into the silence. In her mind's eye, she saw his face light up. *This is what I want,* he'd say. *This is the thing for me.*

She never, ever wanted to change him. But the fact remained that opening one door meant closing another. He wrestled with that nightly. And every time another email or call came in from a record label A&R scout asking what he was working on these days and if he wanted to maybe do a show or two, she saw that it pained her fiancé to say no. To say, "I'm a family man now."

"Whoa!" came a sudden cry from the kitchen. "Liza, get in here!"

The shock interruption of her thoughts sent her heart leaping into her throat. Her brain immediately went to dark places. *Winter fell and got hurt. Oliver sliced his finger off chopping potatoes. There's a gas leak in the house; it's about to explode.* She raced into the kitchen, ready for the sight of blood and gore.

But it was just Oliver bent over the kitchen counter with the newspaper spread out in front of him. Winter was playing contentedly at his feet, babbling to herself. He glanced up at her as she came skidding in. His eyes were wide in surprise. He waved her over urgently.

"You scared me!" she snapped. "Don't do that!"

He chuckled and whistled low in surprise. "Trust me, babe. You're gonna want to see this."

Frowning, she walked around and looked over his shoulder to see the article in the business section he was pointing at.

Prominent Goldman Sachs VP Arrested, read the headline.

She gasped. "No way."

Clay Reeves, the Executive Vice President for Customer Relations of the Goldman Sachs Leveraged Finance Capital Markets group, was arrested today in a joint FBI-SEC sting on charges of embezzlement, wire fraud, and possession of Schedule I narcotics, the article began. *Sources say Reeves acted alone in appropriating several million dollars' worth of firm revenue into private offshore accounts. These illicit gains funded a lavish lifestyle, including the purchase and distribution of cocaine and methamphetamine, according to court documents obtained by investigators.*

Eliza couldn't believe what she was seeing. The article went into further detail describing Clay's crimes. But the gist of it was that her ex-fiancé was almost certainly going to jail for a very, very long time.

She looked up to Oliver, eyes wide. He whistled again. "That puts an end to that mess," he said quietly.

She knew exactly what he meant. "That mess" referred to the ugly underbelly of the last year—Clay's intermittent attempts to seize custody of her daughter. He'd had a lawyer send a nasty, threatening letter demanding visitation and a co-parenting arrangement in which Winter would spend time with both Eliza and her biological father. Eliza, with the help of her brother-in-law Pete, who was a lawyer, had fought off the advances as best as she could. Fortunately, Clay didn't seem to be too consistent with his threats, because he'd follow up one aggressive demand with months of radio silence before resurfacing.

Now, though, that disturbing saga was over. Clay was in jail. That meant no more threatening letters. No more custody battle.

It was over.

She put her arms around Oliver and her head against his chest. She fingered her engagement ring behind her back as she just breathed and relaxed in his embrace.

Things were going to be good from here on out. She just knew it. Her wedding was in seven days. Her soon-to-be-husband loved her and wanted to provide for her and their daughter. Her ex was no longer in the picture.

It was going to be a very good week indeed.

Who cared if wedding planning was hard? Who cared if motherhood was hard? This—this hug, this smell, this warm and beautiful moment—this would always be easy.

3

BRENT

Monday morning.
Six days until Eliza's wedding.

~

Brent Benson drummed his fingers on the steering wheel and sang along to Bruce Springsteen's "Born in the USA" on the truck radio. It used to be one of his dad's favorite songs. Back in the day, whenever it came on, his dad would crank the volume and sing at the top of his lungs in what had to be one of the worst singing voices ever forced upon the world. It was god-awful. Cringeworthy. Nails on a chalkboard.

And yet, Brent would've given everything he had to hear his dad singing just one more time.

That was life, though. Brent had learned—albeit very, very slowly—over the last two years how to just sit with his hurt, with his grief, instead of letting it take him over. He remained a work in progress, to be sure. But it was better than it once was.

That was Rose's doing, no doubt. She knew all the telltale signs of an incoming rain cloud in Brent's heart. She was so good at breaking up the patterns. She'd touch him gently on the wrist and look him in the face with those honey-gold eyes. "Brent," she'd say in a voice that was somehow soft and piercing at the same time. "Breathe."

He pulled into the parking lot and hopped out of his truck. As he strode towards the front doors of Nantucket Elementary School, he was still humming along to the Springsteen song. He had a sudden flashback to years and years ago, when he was just a little boy.

"Dad," he'd asked, *"how does the radio work?"*

His dad had explained about invisible radio waves surging through the air . He said the radio had a special ear, a very sensitive one, that could hear those invisible waves. And then the radio would sing along to those waves so that normal people could hear what they were saying.

Brent smiled at the memory. That was just like his father. A little bit right, a little bit wrong, but absolutely unforgettable. He himself would be twenty-five years old in just a few months, and he certainly knew more about the world than he had when his father was explaining the secrets of the radio. Yet there was still a part of his heart that believed the radio with its special ear was singing out loud so everybody could have a chance to hear it. What a nice little machine.

He chuckled under his breath. This, it turned out, was an awfully funny part of growing up: realizing that not everything worked in quite the way his father had explained it to him. Why, Dad had once told him that potato chips were so crunchy because they had little bits of cockroach in them! Young Brent had squealed in horror and sworn off potato chips for almost ten years before he realized that Dad was just messing with him. That memory made him laugh, too.

He was still laughing as he stepped inside into the air-conditioned coolness of the building. "Good morning, Vivian," he said politely to the secretary behind the desk at the school's entrance. "Think you could wrangle me a visitor's badge? I'm just popping in for a quick visit."

Vivian smiled. She was a nice woman in her early forties with cherry-red hair and cornflower blue eyes. Brent always swore that she looked like the Wendy's logo.

He couldn't wait to see the look on Rose's face when he surprised her in just a minute. He'd finished up today's tasks at his current work site faster than expected this morning. So, with a couple of hours to kill, he'd decided to come by her kindergarten classroom. He'd stopped by the florist on the way over and picked up a bouquet of roses. Roses for Rose. A little trite, maybe, but you couldn't fault the gesture.

Brent smiled to himself as he collected the visitor's badge from Vivian and thanked her. Rose was really bringing out the cheeseball in him these days. They'd gone to the freaking pumpkin patch last fall, for crying out loud! Him, her, and her adorable little girl, Susanna, all decked out in matching plaid shirts, doing hay rides and a pumpkin carving contest and all manner of autumn activities. And he'd loved every second of it.

Oh, how things had changed.

He rounded the corner at the end of the hallway and saw the door to Rose's classroom. It was festooned with ribbons and stickers in bright summer colors. The school year would be over at the end of this week, so he'd figured that now was as good a time as any to drop by unannounced. The door was slightly ajar. Flowers in hand, he nudged it open and stuck his head in.

He held his breath for a second while he took in the scene. Rose was seated at the front of the classroom on a small stool, reading to the students, who were gathered in a tight-knit semicircle around her. Every single one of the kids was listening with bated breath to a story about a lost little elephant and his friend, the mischievous monkey.

Brent felt his heart pick up a beat. Maybe "cheeseball" wasn't even doing him justice anymore. He was a level beyond that, even.

"Knock knock," he said playfully when Rose paused to turn the page. Her eyes shot up from the book. When she saw who it was at her door, a huge grin broke out across her face.

She had her hair pulled back in a bun, with crisscrossed pencils piercing through it. Brent loved it. He always teased her, asking if they taught teachers how to do that on day one of job orientation. That usually earned him a swat on the shoulder and a roll of the eyes. She was wearing a long green sun dress and her feet were bare. She looked like a summer princess, a fairy, something out of a dream, something too good to be true. Too good to be his.

And yet, she was.

"Boys and girls," she announced, "can you all say hello to Mr. B?"

Twenty pairs of eyes swiveled over to him. "Hello, Mr. B!" they all chorused in unison.

"I brought flowers," he said, brandishing the bouquet.

Rose's eyes lit up. "Who's the lucky lady?"

Brent turned to the class. "Do you guys think I should give these to Miss Bowman?"

"Yes!" screeched the girls, at the same time all the boys yelled, "Ew, no!"

He laughed. Rose accepted the flowers with a modest little curtsy. "I'm going to go put these in some water so they stay nice and strong," she said. "Mr. B, would you mind taking over?" She handed him the book.

"With pleasure, Miss Bowman." He settled onto the stool that Rose had just vacated. "Now, where were we …"

He picked up the story where she'd left off. He gave the elephant a special voice—slow, thoughtful, calm—and the same for the monkey, who was a little more of a chatterbox, at least in Brent's version of things. The kids stayed clustered around him. They giggled and gasped at all the right moments.

The time wound by slowly as Brent read the rest of the story. When he was all done, with a big, dramatic, *"And they all lived happily ever after. The End!"*, he closed the book with a snap. Rose had taken up a seat on the carpet in the back, her legs swept over to one side as she gazed up at him with stars in her eyes.

"Class, can we give Mr. B a round of applause to thank him for reading to us?" she asked. The kids all clapped politely. Brent gave a modest bow as Rose took to her feet and circled around to the front. "Excellent manners, thank you. All right, time for activity rotations! Green group, please stand up." About a quarter of the kids took to their feet. "You all can start this afternoon at the book station." A few of the kids jumped up and down excitedly, then they all took off towards one corner of the classroom, where bins full of colorful books awaited them. Rose dismissed the rest of the groups one at a time to the different areas—seat work, arts and crafts, and toys. When they were all happily occupied, she turned back to Brent.

"Who invited you, mister?" she murmured playfully with a little jab in his chest.

He grinned. "Just thought I'd surprise my favorite teacher, that's all."

"I'd *better* be your favorite."

"It was close between you and Mrs. Greenfield. She's cuter, but you cook me dinner sometimes, so I gave it to you in the tiebreaker round."

Rose had to muffle a laugh at that. Mrs. Greenfield was as nice as could be, but she was as old as could be, too. "The Dinosaur of Nantucket Elementary," went the teasing nickname. She'd be the first one to fire off a self-deprecating joke, though, so it wasn't like Brent was being cruel or anything.

"Speaking of dinner," Brent continued, "what's on the menu tonight?"

"Again, very presumptuous, sir," Rose poked back. "You keep showing up places you aren't invited."

"You wound me, madam," he said, holding a hand over his heart like it was broken. "But tell me it's lasagna, and all will be well in the world again."

Rose smiled, her eyes sparkling. "It might be. And there might be apple pie afterwards, if you play your cards right."

"You're the best."

"Don't I know it."

"Mrs. Bowman!" one of the kids called from the corner. "Can you help me?"

"Duty calls," Rose said to Brent regretfully.

"Actually," he said, "I've still got an hour or so before I gotta be anywhere. Mind if I stick around and play?"

Rose tilted her head to the side and looked at him with a soft smile playing at the corner of her lips. "I'd like that."

Rolling up his sleeves, Brent went off to rescue the student in the arts-and-crafts corner from the perilous glue-stick trap they were ensnared in, smiling broadly all the while. He spent the rest of the afternoon rotating around with the kids, sounding out tough words, practicing math, building block towers.

The smile never let his face for even a second.

∼

Monday night.

"Mama, can I be excused?" Susanna asked.

Rose glanced over at her six-year-old daughter's plate. "Did you finish all your vegetables?"

"Yes!"

Brent tried his best to suppress his laughter. Susanna had been feeding the cat green beans since the moment they sat down. But he wasn't going to be the one to snitch on her, so he just focused on his lasagna and kept his face down towards his dish.

Rose looked suspicious of her daughter, but without any evidence to detain her, she nodded. "All right then, you can go."

Susanna scampered off before she could be subjected to any further questioning. Brent took a big sip of water until his laughter finally settled down.

"Delicious, as always," he said when he'd cleaned his plate.

"Thanks, boo," Rose replied.

"I'll wash, you dry?"

"Tell you what: you do both, and I'll sit and watch you with a glass of wine."

Brent groaned and rolled his eyes. "Once again, I draw the short straw. My life is nothing but suffering."

"Quit being a drama queen," she reprimanded as she picked up her plate and walked around the table towards the kitchen. She stopped and kissed him on the top of the head on her way.

Laughing, Brent cleared the table and took it all over to the sink to start washing up. True to her word, Rose poured a small glass of chardonnay and hopped up on the edge of the counter.

"You sure you want to do this?" she asked after a moment.

He looked up at her. He was still smiling, but it was a serious kind of smile. A *yes, duh* kind of smile.

"This" was something they had been discussing for a few months now: the prospect of moving in together.

Ever since the night a year ago when Brent had come to Rose in the pouring rain and said he couldn't let her go, they'd been careful about their newfound relationship. They took each step delicately. One kiss at a time, one night at a time. Rose was wary of Susanna's feelings—it wasn't good to have a man flitting in and out of her daughter's life, here one day and gone the next. She was wary of her own heart, too. Brent knew that. His feelings weren't exactly the most durable at the moment, either. But there was a real kind of beauty in moving slowly together, in treating each other like fragile glass. This was the biggest step yet, but he was as sure of it as he had been the moment he first kissed her.

He wanted this. He wanted her. He wanted them.

"I'm sure," he answered.

She nodded slowly as she gazed into the distance. Brent scrubbed a few dishes and set them out to dry.

"What's on your mind?" His hands stayed busy.

"Thinking about you," she answered at once.

"Oh yeah? What about me?"

He felt her eyes shift onto him, and he could hear the sly grin in her voice. "You were great with the kids today."

His face burned at that. He wasn't exactly sure why. It felt like there was more to that comment than the mere fact that he'd hung out with a motley crew of five- and six-year-olds for an afternoon. If there *was* in fact a deeper meaning to Rose's innocent comment, he knew what it might refer to.

Would they have kids together one day?

To be perfectly honest, the thought had never even occurred to Brent. He was young in years at twenty-four, but he felt like he'd lived so much during that time. The last three years alone had aged him at double the normal rate at least. Everything about his life now had a different vibe to it than what he thought of as a "normal" mid-twenties lifestyle. He had a serious girlfriend, a business. He was a father of sorts to a young girl who looked up to him. Nothing was normal. But nothing was out of place, either.

Henrietta, his dog, came up and nipped at his hand where it hung by his side. He looked down at her. She always knew when he was thinking deep thoughts. There was a skeptical look on her face right now. It was almost reassuring, in a strange way, although he knew he was almost certainly projecting. Henrietta alternated most of the time between hungry and sleepy. The nuances of fatherhood and a man's responsibility to his family weren't exactly in her wheelhouse.

And yet, he felt like she understood him at least as much as anybody. She sensed his fear, his hope. She saw what he wanted for himself and for his future. So, when she licked his hand, he looked down at her, and something in her face said, *It's okay.*

That felt good, for reasons he didn't know how to say out loud.

He glanced up and met Rose's gaze. "Thanks," he said with a smile. "I liked hanging out with them."

There was something significant in that answer, too.

4

SARA

Monday night.
Six days until Eliza's wedding.

"So how much are you gonna miss me?" Sara asked Joey.

"Hmm ..." he said, scratching his chin and pretending to weigh the question in his head. "How many stars are there in the sky?"

"It better be more than that."

"Grains of sand on the beach?"

"Better, but still not good enough."

"As much as Joanie loves Chachi?"

Sara groaned and punched him in the shoulder. "That reference is way too old for me, so I know for a fact that it's too old for you, ya whippersnapper."

Joey laughed as he pulled into the parking lot of Sara's restaurant, Little Bull. "You're right. I honestly have no idea what it means."

"Add it to the list."

He popped a finger in his mouth, then aimed it towards Sara's ear, trying to give her a wet willy. She shrieked with laughter and ducked away from him towards the passenger side of the car. "Joey, get that thing away from me right this second!" she squealed.

He sagged back in his seat, chuckling.

"You are a *child*," she said, shaking her head. "I swear. A child."

"Then we know for sure you're a cradle robber," he responded with a twinkle in his eye.

Sara groaned for a second time. "Don't remind me," she said. "Jose has already started purring every time I walk into the kitchen. *The cougar,* he calls me. I've had more flattering nicknames in my lifetime, lemme tell you."

Sara didn't actually care that she was thirty-one to Joey's twenty-seven years old. He was an old soul, wet willies aside. Other twenty-seven-year-olds were still out prowling the bars in Nantucket, looking for easy fun. But Joey liked working—he was a firefighter—and hanging out with Sara at the apartment they shared. They both spent a lot of time at their respective jobs, so they valued the quiet time they could finagle together, just the two of them. Cuddling on the couch and watching a movie, playing cards, stuff like that. Simple little moments of laughter and conversation. Sometimes not even that. Sometimes they just sat with each other and enjoyed being with another person who didn't expect much from them other than the steadiness of a heartbeat, a warm hand, a soft kiss.

Ask Sara from three years ago if she thought she'd end up in a relationship like this and she'd have laughed in your face. Sara 1.0, as she'd started to refer to her past self, wanted to get drunk in a speakeasy in New York City with her fellow chefs. She wanted to get in trouble with the wrong guys, wake up with a hangover and hazy memories, then do it all again the next night.

That Sara was long gone.

Sara 2.0 was night-and-day different. Sara 2.0 was a business owner who said things like, "I'd better get to bed early; I have to do taxes in the morning." Sara 2.0 separated her recycling out and sent her employees handwritten notes on their birthdays. Sara 2.0 volunteered at the food bank with her mother and showed up at town council meetings to vote on new traffic and parking ordinances. Sara 2.0 was reliable, responsible, boring.

And she was living her best life.

"You nervous?" Joey asked her.

Sara gulped. "No," she declared defiantly. She looked over to him and blushed. "Okay, yes. Very."

Tonight would be the debut of a new main course at Little Bull. The dish had a long history, dating all the way back to Sara's earliest experiments during her stint at the Culinary Institute of America. Pulled pork and clams atop Spanish orzo with a gremolata of sundried tomatoes and pineapple. She was well aware that it sounded foul. In fact, everyone she'd described it to over the years had nearly yakked in response. But there was something in it that kept her coming back. Sara had continued toying with it during idle moments despite others' reactions. She never put much stock in other people's opinions, anyway.

Over the last few months it had started to come together, almost by accident. She'd had a dream about it one night and woken up sweating, terrified that she would forget the magical breakthrough that was going to make the dish sing. The next morning, she'd put the new fix into play, and it came out beautifully. One by one, she made her chefs try it, until they all agreed that it was flawless, bold, perfect. Tonight would be its unveiling to the outside world—or to the four dozen lucky diners at Little Bull, at least.

No matter how many times she did this, though, she still got nervous. There was an intensely personal aspect to the kind of cuisine Sara made. She had more in common with an artist than a line cook. The things that came out of her kitchen were memories in the form of food. The brininess of a mouthful of Nantucket ocean water when you wiped out while surfing in the summertime. The sweet tang of cherry popsicles at the fair. When people ate her food, she wanted them to feel like they'd lived her childhood along with her. Or, better yet, for it to speak to their own lives. Everyone brought their individual story to the table at Little Bull. That's what made it special —food was a language for conversation between perfect strangers.

"It's gonna be great, you know," Joey consoled her.

Sara rolled her eyes. "You're required to say that."

"I am not," he replied, mock-offended. When she fixed him with a glare, he admitted, "Okay, fine, yes, I am. But I'm not saying it because I have to. I'm saying it because I know it's gonna be great. That's all. Boy Scouts' honor."

"Were you even a Boy Scout?"

"For about three weeks," he said with a straight face. "I lost at the wooden stock car races, so I cried and smashed my car. My dad made me quit after that."

"Classic JoJo," Sara chuckled. "Sore loser."

"Says the one who flipped over the Monopoly board literally a week ago when you landed on my Park Place hotel three times in a row."

"You cheated!" Sara exclaimed. "Loaded dice! You switched the cards! Witchcraft and wizardry! *Something!*"

He laughed and shook his head sadly, as if to say, *What am I gonna do with you?*

Sara smiled back, then checked her watch. "Shoot, I'm gonna be late. Wish me luck."

"Luck," Joey said, leaning over to kiss her.

"It's supposed to be *good luck*," she admonished.

He paused with his lips just a millimeter away from hers. "Well, you should've specified."

"I shouldn't reward this kind of sass with a kiss."

He pecked her on the lips before she could pull away. "Too late," he said with a grin as he straightened up. "Now go on, scoot. You're not the only one with work to do."

She grinned. "One more kiss first."

He rolled his eyes, but leaned forward and gave her what she asked for.

Satisfied and buzzing with the warmth of his lips on hers, Sara unbuckled, popped open the door of Joey's truck, and hopped out. "I'll be by later to get you," Joey called out from the driver's seat.

"You better," she teased.

"On second thought, maybe I won't."

"No leftovers for you, then!"

He hit the steering wheel in mock frustration. "You've got me over a barrel there. Guess I'll be here after all. Later, sunshine." He blew her another kiss. Then she turned and walked into her restaurant.

Cassandra, the former head hostess who had recently been promote to maître' d, gave her a friendly smile and wave as Sara swept in.

"Any special requests tonight?" Sara asked as she set her stuff down in her office.

"For a change, not a single one," Cassandra answered after checking the evening's reservations in the online system. "Word on the street is that you're debuting a new dish. The people are clamoring for details."

"They'll know soon enough," Sara responded with a cheeky smile. *Assuming this tasting goes well.*

The rest of the staff—mostly front-of-the-house folks and the prep chefs, those who weren't involved in the menu creation processes—was going to try the pork and clams dish tonight. If that went well, the dish would go to the restaurant's guests. If it bombed—well, Sara would figure something out.

After getting settled into her office, Sara went around and stuck her head in the kitchen. It was abuzz with activity as each of the chefs got their mise-en-place set for the evening and finished the final stages of prep. They had about forty-five minutes until first seating, so Sara would need to do the tasting and brief the servers on the new dish in T-minus twenty. Time was ticking away.

She searched the room until she found Jose, her right-hand man, standing in a corner at the back. He was a blur of activity, chopping, whipping, tasting, repeat. When he looked up a moment later and saw her standing there, he waved her over urgently.

Sara made her way over, doing the delicate dance required to move through a professional kitchen without causing absolute disaster. It took precise timing to avoid crashing into each other. But that was one of the things she loved about this environment. There was a place for everything and a thing for every place. A sense of belonging radiated everywhere; order amidst the chaos. It was beautiful in its own way.

When she came up to Jose, he looked grim. "Talk to me," she ordered. "You know I don't like it when you get all serious like that."

He fidgeted, sighed, shook his head like a wet dog, scratched his thick beard. "It's just ... It's not working." He looked up at her. "It's the worst thing I've ever tasted in my life."

Sara felt crushed. Flattened, actually, like fresh dough that someone had worked for hours with a rolling pin. They'd have to pull the plug on the star dish of the night then. The diners would be disappointed. Maybe there was a reviewer in attendance tonight who'd been looking forward to something innovative ...

She glanced up at Jose again and saw him grinning.

"Jose," she said in a warning tone. "If you're messing with me ..."

His smile split wider and he started to laugh. It was a real belly laugh, the kind that started from deep within and blossomed outwards until he was laughing with every part of his body, slapping his knees, wiping tears from his eyes. Like Santa Claus, if Santa Claus was from Guatemala.

"*Chica,* I'm kidding, I'm kidding! It's perfect. You are a genius. A genius, *cierto.*"

Sara's first reaction was to grab a wooden spoon from a cup nearby and whack him over the head with it. He laughed and shielded himself, ducking, as she whaled on him a few times.

"I! Told! You! Don't! Do! That!"

After a few solid connections, she was laughing, too. The rest of the kitchen looked over, wondering what on earth was going on. Sara's crestfallen feeling had disappeared, swept away by the fist-pumping euphoria of nailing something difficult. She found a tasting spoon nearby and took a bite of the plate that Jose had assembled.

The flavors exploded in her mouth. The salty fattiness of the pork, with that sweet smoke lingering in the background, worked so well with the deep ocean deliciousness of the clams. The orzo soaked it all up and magnified it ten times over, adding layers of depth like bass notes to a melody. The twin bursts of sun-dried tomato and pineapple were playful, unexpected, surprising, and yet so perfect that it was like they'd been created specifically to go together.

It was a smash hit in the making.

She hollered for everyone to come over and join her. The crew fell in at once, circling up around her. She told someone to go get the front-of-house gang, too. A moment later, she had her entire staff of twenty-one standing at crisp attention around her.

It was impossible to keep the smile off her face as she gave them the rundown on the dish. She'd already planned out how she wanted them to describe it to their guests, how to plate it, how to present it. She ran through the details one by one, luxuriating in the booming "Yes, chef!" that resounded from her assembled employees every time she asked if they understood.

Then, briefing complete, she got out of the way so that Jose could distribute the tasting sample to each of them. It was important to Sara that her servers and chefs knew firsthand what they were offering to their guests. How else could they make diners feel like a part of the environment? Everyone was on an equal footing at Little Bull, because without any single one of them, the place wasn't complete. Sara had always loved that about restaurants. At good ones, at least, there was no such thing as more or less important. They were all essential, from the head chef down to the greenest dishwasher.

Sara turned away to answer a few questions for one of the newer members of the serving crew. When she turned back around, she was stunned to see her boyfriend bringing up the rear of the tasting line. Joey had his mouth full already. He gave her a big thumbs-up and a smile when he saw that she had noticed him.

"What happened to '*You're not the only one with work to do?*'" she teased with her hands on her hips.

He shrugged. "I like listening to you be the boss," he explained. "So I just snuck in the back for a sec. And when I heard there were samples to be had, I couldn't resist. Sue me. This is amazing, by the way. Pineapple and tomatoes. Who woulda thunk it?"

Sara laughed and swatted him with a dish towel, just like her mother had done to her for her entire life. "You like everything."

He nodded solemnly. "Guilty as charged."

She kissed him on the cheek. "It's one of your best qualities. Now get out of my kitchen, civilian, before I do something drastic."

"You're always about to do something drastic," Joey called over his shoulder as he sauntered out of the kitchen, licking his lips. "It's one of *your* best qualities!"

Then he was gone, leaving her laughing. She surveyed the kitchen. Everyone had returned to work at once. She was standing in the middle of a hive of activity. It was chaotic, it was beautiful, it was perfect.

It was hers.

5

HOLLY

It was dinnertime at the Goodwin household. This time of year, Mondays meant meatloaf, which was just about ready to come out of the oven.

"Grady, did you wash your hands?" Holly asked her son as he went to sit down at the dining room table.

"Mhmm," he mumbled nonchalantly.

"Show me."

He hesitated for just a second. That was all the answer she needed. "Up. Go. Scrub good, twenty seconds at least." The guilty party slunk off towards the kitchen sink. Holly glanced towards her daughter, Alice, who was already ensconced in her seat across the table. The seven-year-old waggled her freshly scrubbed fingertips at her mom. She'd painted each of them a different color, courtesy of the at-home nail salon that Aunt Sara had gotten her as a Christmas gift.

Pete came sliding into the dining room right on cue, propping his briefcase up against a wall and loosening his tie as he took his seat.

Holly walked around and set the tray with the meatloaf on the lazy Susan in the center of the table. "Bon appetit," she said.

"Looks great, babe," Pete said at once. He was licking his lips.

Grady slipped back into his seat, hands scrubbed and soapy, though Holly noticed a few nails that could've used a little bit more TLC. Oh well. There was only so much a mother could do with a nine-year-old boy, especially a rough-and-tumble type like her firstborn.

"How was work, Daddy?" asked Alice.

"It was good, darling. Thanks for asking."

"Ready to be out of that place?" Holly inquired.

For the last year, Pete and his partner in his new venture, Billy Payne, had been working out of a conference room at a property owned by one of Pete's high school buddies. It was only meant to be a temporary solution—cut costs while the law firm got up and running —but it had gone on a little bit longer than either one of them had ever intended.

Gradually, though, they'd won enough business to start looking around for office space of their own. Just last week, they'd found the perfect site. It was actually an old firehouse that was no longer in use. With some small renovations and a thorough redecoration, it was going to be a lovely little space for the two of them to work, host clients, and—one day—hire in new employees.

"You don't even know the half of it." Pete sighed as he devoured his plate of meatloaf and green beans. "I will forever be grateful to Ethan for letting us camp out at his place. But if I have to smell his secretary's god-awful perfume one more time, I'm gonna lose it. I swear, it's like she sprays a skunk on herself every morning."

Grady cackled maniacally at that. Holly just shook her head and chewed thoughtfully. The boys in her family were two peas in a pod, always getting into trouble together and cracking each other up. She thanked the heavens every day that she still had a sweet little mama's girl to see things from her perspective, even if Alice's independent streak only continued to grow with each passing year.

"How was school, kiddo?" Pete asked Grady.

"Good!" Grady chirped. "We made rockets. Mine went the highest."

"Did you do what I said with the fins? Those instructions the manufacturers give out are always wrong. The secret is ..." The two of them went off on a tangent about optimal rocket ship design while Holly and Alice rolled their eyes and looked at each other knowingly. She might only be seven, but Alice already had that "*Men—what're we gonna do with them?*" look down pat. It made Holly laugh every time.

"How was your day, sweetie?" Holly asked.

"It was fine," Alice answered. She was stirring the peas on her plate around with a fork, not eating much. "Lila and Jillian were being mean, though, so I didn't really hang out with them."

"Mean to you?"

"Just mean. They're not nice sometimes." Alice had a way of retreating within herself sometimes that was starting to worry Holly a little bit. There was a kind of world-weariness about her when she was down. Every now and then, she mentioned something about missing Grandpa. That took Holly by surprise. Alice had been so young when her grandfather passed away. It didn't seem like she ought to have been quite so affected. But evidently there was a little grain of sadness still tucked away in her heart somewhere. Just something to watch, that's all. Not every kid grew up in a smooth, straight line. And even the ones who seemed like they did often turned out to need a little bit of remedial self-care later in life. Just look at Eliza, Holly's oldest sister. She'd aced the first thirty years of her life with flying colors. But she'd pretty much undergone a complete reset in the last two or three years. The wedding this weekend would be a culmination of that whole process. A new Eliza, a new name, a new life. Holly smiled at the thought of her big sister's happiness. Weddings always made Holly giddy. She loved love.

"Oh! I forgot," Pete said after dinner, when the kids had been cut loose and the two of them were washing up together. Pete was a fastidious scrubber of dishes. He drove Holly nuts sometimes with how carefully he went over each one, again and again, examining it from every angle until he was sure the thing was spotless. He cared about the dishes so much, and yet the entire concept of folding clothes before putting them in the dresser drawer seemed to have missed him completely.

"Forgot what?"

"I talked to Billy today, and we're all cool with you taking lead on the office décor stuff. That's your cup of tea anyway. Neither of us are much good at it."

Holly set down the pan she was drying and squealed. "Really? Yay! Aw, honey, thank you. I'm so excited."

The question of who got to decorate the office had been lingering over her head for the better part of a year now, pretty much ever since she and Pete had moved from Plymouth, Massachusetts, to Nantucket so Pete could start this new law firm. It had almost been waged like a proxy war between Holly and Billy's wife, Cecilia, who was a witchy woman if ever there was one. They interacted as minimally as possible. After the dual shock of discovering that her dream house had been snatched out from under her and learning that the woman responsible was the wife of her husband's new business partner, Holly had been determined to steer clear of Cecilia Payne.

The night of that twin discovery had been a doozy to say the least. They'd gone to the debut night of Holly's sister's new restaurant and proceeded to have what was easily the most awkward dinner of Holly's life. She couldn't get out of there fast enough. By the time the meal was close to over, she'd made at least half a dozen trips to the bathroom, just to escape the oppressive atmosphere that hung over their table. Billy and Pete were completely oblivious at the time, of course. Pete had treated the whole house theft affair as an "Aw, bummer " kind of thing. Holly couldn't possibly disagree more with that. This wasn't "Aw, bummer." This was a high crime and misdemeanor. A mortal sin. What kind of punishment Cecilia deserved, Holly couldn't say for sure, but she definitely shouldn't get off scot-free.

Pete, for his part, had done his best to calm Holly down. The best way to do that seemed to be to just keep the two women far apart. Fine, fair enough. Out of sight, out of mind, as the saying went. Holly had a life to live. She didn't need to devote time or mental energy to that condescending woman.

But then the question of who got to decorate their husbands' new office had emerged. Holly had gathered from little things that Pete had mentioned here and there that Cecilia once had a small interior design business a few years ago. Nothing super professional or notable. It seemed, though, that Cecilia felt that her experience in that area made her the obvious choice to handle the décor.

The problem was, Holly wanted to take charge of it. She'd been a stay-at-home mother for so long—nine years now! She badly craved a project. Something big, something fun, something new. This would fit the bill perfectly. And she loved the spot they'd chosen. The layout of the old firehouse meant there were so many fun, quirky things she could do with the space. Her mind had started whirling from the moment she'd first set foot in what was soon going to be the office of Goodwin & Payne Law Firm.

So hearing Pete say the project was hers was a big, big victory, small as it might seem in the grand scheme of things. She kissed her husband on the cheek, still squirming with excitement, and ran off to the second bedroom they used as an office to start sketching out her ideas.

6

SARA

The Monday night dinner service at Little Bull was over, and Sara had retreated to her office. She closed her eyes and leaned back in the wheeled chair behind her desk, letting out a long, exhausted sigh. Outside, she could hear the clink and clatter of tables being cleared, the kitchen being scrubbed down, and the muted gossip of her staff as they put everything away for the night. Inside the office, though, all she could hear was her own breathing.

She wanted to sit and soak in the silence for a minute. It had been a good dinner service. Fabulous, actually. The dish had come out to rave reviews. She hid in a corner and watched each diner take their first bite. She saw their faces twist up in ecstasy, eyes fluttering, cheeks sagging in that *Wow, this is something else* expression that she'd come to cherish and crave so much. She loved watching people eat food she had poured herself into. Each time they took a fresh bite, she got to experience a fraction of that joy with them.

So why the long face?

She knew exactly the reason. It was hiding in her back pocket, folded and tucked away. A well-worn sheet of paper. Her fingers itched. She wanted to reach back there and retrieve it, unfold it across her desk and read it for the billionth time. She started to move her hand towards her pocket and—

No.

Not tonight. *Don't do it, Sara.* Don't give in to the stupid, self-hating temptation. Tonight was good. Tonight was successful. Tonight was a win.

Let it go.

She leaned forward and planted her elbows heavily on her desk. It wobbled a little bit—she'd been meaning to get Joey in here to fix the one leg that was shorter than all the others, but it kept slipping her mind. Rubbing the heels of her hands into her tired eyeballs, she let out one more long sigh before turning her attention to the stacks of paper lined up on her desk.

The numbers painted a clear story. Little Bull, against all odds, was doing just fine. It wasn't a gold mine just yet, but nor was it a money pit. There was a clear route to financial success if they just kept doing the things they'd been doing since the day they opened: pleasing customers one bite at a time. She was proud of the systems she'd put in the place, the staff she'd trained, the menu she had sweated over until it was as perfect as she knew how to make it. And, night after night, that work was rewarded. With smiles, with *mmm*s, with laughter.

She spent a few minutes shuffling through the stacks of invoices and budget reports. There were food shipments to order, lease payments to schedule, special reservation requests to approve. Just the million and one little tasks of drudgery that filled the life of a new business owner. Sara didn't mind. Honestly, she found herself liking this part of the job. Every time she finished a task, she got the satisfaction of saying to herself, *That's done now.* It was so unlike the art of cooking, which involved two steps forward and ten steps back over and over. This was straightforward, rote, systematic. She turned her brain into a spreadsheet and let the numbers populate the cells. In that way, she forgot for long stretches of time about the paper tucked in her back pocket.

But tonight, the magic spell of busywork wasn't doing such a good job at keeping her distracted. Her fingers still tingled to reach back and pluck the sheet from her pocket. She knew what it said, of course—she'd memorized every single word on the printout months and months ago. It wasn't about being reminded of its contents. It was a ritual. A destructive one, and yet one that she didn't know how to quit.

After reading over the same itemized line on a kitchen equipment invoice fifteen times in a row, she growled in frustration, gave up, and yanked the paper out of her back pocket.

Her hands were trembling as she started to read the words she'd read a million times already and would no doubt read at least a million more before this sheet gave up the ghost and just straight-up crumbled into dust.

Arrogance Meets Incompetence in New Nantucket Wannabe, the headline read. Next to the byline was the smug, unsmiling face of Martin Hogan, the country's preeminent food critic.

Sara's stomach churned.

But she couldn't stop. Once she got going, it was like an addiction. She knew how she was going to feel by the time she finished reading Hogan's review. It just wasn't enough to make her put it away before it hurt her one more time.

In thirty-plus years of sampling the best this country's chefs have to offer, it has been thankfully rare that I have to plant such a blatant "You Shall Not Pass" in the path of a young culinary artist. And yet, such is my unfortunate responsibility after spending a misbegotten evening in the gastronomical care of upstart chef Sara Benson, founder and creative driving force behind Nantucket's Little Bull restaurant. For those of you without the stomach to read about the gross crimes committed on good taste under Chef Benson's watch, I suggest you read no further. You need to know only this: it is an offense to your palate to ever frequent this establishment.

If you are still with me, let us embark on our tour through the Little Bull "House of Horrors"...

Sara stopped reading for a second. Right on schedule, there was a tear leaking from one eye down her cheek. That only happened some of the times when she subjected herself this savage, brutal hit job. Other times, she got mad. Mad enough to break things. Snapped-in-half pens and pencils filled her office trash can on a regular basis. The broken short leg on the desk was her fault, after maybe the twentieth or thirtieth time she had pored over Hogan's words. Tonight, though, was apparently destined to be a sad, self-pitying night.

She knew this was her fault. Sort of, that is. She'd been offered a way out of this swamp, and she'd chosen to reject it.

The thing was, she stood by that decision. Her mind flashed back to that night a year ago when Gavin Crawford, her old boss and sort-of flame, had shown up unexpectedly at Little Bull with his good pal Martin Hogan tagging along for the ride. It was only a few short months after Gavin had wrecked her life for the second time. Bad things came in threes, apparently.

Gavin had given her the choice: come see him in his hotel room that night, or face the wrath of a nationally published food critic set loose to tear Sara's hopes and dreams to shreds. She'd weighed her options, but at the end of the night, she'd spit in Gavin's face—metaphorically speaking. Actually, now that she thought about it, she wished she'd done that literally. Gavin deserved it. He didn't know how to leave her alone. She was "the one that got away," but in less of a Hallmark lovey-dovey sense and more of a serial-killer-whose-victim-has-escaped kind of way. Like he had seen her living her best life away from him and thought to himself, *"My collection isn't complete without her in it."* Beneath his pretty boy smile and overly full trophy shelf, Gavin Crawford was a smug jerk and a narcissist. If only she'd seen that a long time ago. Before it was too late.

Now, she just had to take the damage and keep on keeping on. What else was there to do? It wasn't like she could accuse Gavin of pulling strings to get Martin to slander her, even if everyone involved knew that that's exactly what happened. No one cared about her version of events, no matter how true it was.

She didn't have to keep reading to know what the rest of the article said.

... unholy chimera of over-acidity and so much salt that I almost wondered if they'd accidentally dropped my dish in the harbor before serving it to me ...

... foul concoction, utterly lacking in nuance and craft ...

... My grandmother would roll over in her grave if she could see how this poor lobster had been mangled and maligned ...

It went on like that, each line worse than the last, until the very end: *If she has any sense of humility at all—which would seem like a dubious proposition at best—she will close up shop and apologize to her betters at once.*

Boom. Kill shot. A dagger to the heart.

Sara let the sheet fall from her hand onto the desk. The tear on her cheek fell with it.

She herself hadn't always been the nicest of girls. In middle school, she'd told Mary Claire McGuire that her nose looked like a carrot. Once, she'd lied to a professor at culinary school about a tree branch falling onto her car in order to duck out of an exam she didn't study for. She regularly snuck candy into the movie theater.

But no one deserved to be treated like this.

How Little Bull managed to continue operations despite the heat of Hogan's review was beyond Sara. She was glad it had kept chugging along. There were far more interests than just hers at stake. Her father's life insurance payout was what had enabled this dream to take root in the first place. That, along with the hard work of her family and her staff, were all crucial factors in getting Little Bull up and running.

She had to continue. But on nights like this, when Hogan's words seared into her brain and she could see only Gavin's smug scowl every time she closed her eyes, she felt like doing anything but that.

Sara counted to one hundred, slowly. Then she forced herself to get to her feet. No more self-pitying. She'd had plenty of that for the evening.

Most of the staff had filtered out, leaving only Cassandra and Jose behind. She dismissed them both with a wave of her hand. "I'll see you guys tomorrow night," she murmured. "I'll lock up. Don't worry about it."

They shrugged, bid her good night, and left out the back entrance. Sara picked up her things and followed them out, pulling the door shut and locking it behind her.

She weighed her options. The night was clear and crisp, unusually cool for the time of year, with a nice breeze coming in off the water. She'd told Joey when he dropped her off that she wanted a ride home, but now she was changing her mind. It'd be good to walk the long route back to the apartment they shared.

Maybe the Nantucket night air would clear her mind.

7

BRENT

Tuesday afternoon.
Five days until Eliza's wedding.

∾

Brent and Marshall had taken a group of fraternity brothers on a half-day fishing trip. They'd caught a whole bundle of bluefish, stripers, and bonita, so everybody was in a good mood by the time they made it back to shore.

Brent had made quick work of cleaning Marshall's boat up and getting it back on the trailer. With the success of the charter fishing business over the last year, they'd recently upgraded their craft to *The Tripidation III,* adding another four-stroke motor and eight feet in length, which made for nice fishing and a smooth ride no matter where they went. It also let them take a few more people out at a time, so that had been a nice bump to the bottom line as well.

"Mind if I duck out early?" Brent asked Marshall, his partner and best friend. "I wanna catch Rose on her lunch break."

"Say no more, Triple B!" Marshall replied with his trademark bombast. "Love waits for no man!"

Brent laughed and took off for his truck. His hands were still dripping with saltwater. It was 11:49, according to his watch, and Rose's lunch break ended at 12:05, so he had to hustle if he wanted to get to her in time. It was just a quick jump over from the marina to the school, though, so he was walking through the front doors and waving hello to Vivian again about four minutes later.

"Back so soon?" she asked brightly.

"Can't stay away," he said with a wink. "I'll be right back. Promise not to tell on me?"

"I'll pretend I didn't even see you," she said, winking back.

Brent gave her a smile and thumbs-up and went jogging down the hall towards the cafeteria. It was mayhem inside—kids seated along either side of the long lunch tables, laughing and squealing playfully. Brent spotted Rose at the teachers' table in the far corner. He waved her over urgently. Frowning, she got up and made her way over to him, stopping halfway to separate two kids who were trying to throw grapes into each other's mouths from across the table.

"Everything okay?" she asked with a wrinkled brow when she finally reached him.

"Better than okay," he said. "C'mon. Quick field trip. I have a surprise for you." He grabbed her hand and pulled her through the double doors.

"You gonna tell me what's going on?" she asked, half laughing as he tugged her down the hallway and back out the front doors, waving to Vivian as they exited.

"You'll see when we get there." He opened the passenger door to his truck and helped her in, then went around to his side to fire up the engine. "Buckle your seat belt."

Rose checked her watch. "I have to be back in eleven minutes," she said. "You better drive fast, Mr. NASCAR."

"You got it, princess." He floored the engine and they took off bumping down the road, with the radio cranked up loud and the wind rippling through their hair.

They turned down Howard Street three and a half minutes later and pulled to a stop in front of the house he'd grown up in.

Brent looked over to Rose and grinned. "Surprise," he said.

Her forehead furrowed as she looked around for the surprise. Finally, stumped, she turned back to him. "I don't get it."

He pointed out the window at the house. "That's the surprise."

"What is?"

"*That.*"

"What's in the house?"

He sighed. So much for a storybook moment. "The house *is* the surprise, you turkey."

Rose looked back and forth between him and the house, him and the house. It took three or four double takes before the truth of what he was telling her actually clicked into place. When it did, the color drained from her face. "Brent, you cannot be serious."

His grin spread one notch wider. "Serious as a heart attack, my love."

"You ... you ..."

"... I bought my mom's house," he finished for her. His cheeks hurt from grinning so much, but he couldn't stop it if he tried. "Well," he corrected, "I'm going to buy it. But it's more or less a done deal."

Rose still had no clue what to say. Her mouth was flopping open and shut like a fish out of water.

Laughing, he took mercy on her and explained everything that was going on. Over the last year, as he'd built up his contracting business and taken on an equal partnership with Marshall on the charter fishing trips, he'd been quietly putting away as much money as he could into a secret savings account. It'd been killing him to do it without telling Rose—or any living soul, for that matter. But he knew that an opportunity of some kind was going to pop up sooner or later. So when Mom had started making noise about selling the house on Howard Street now that she and Dominic were the owners of the Sweet Island Inn, he knew that the stars were aligning.

But Brent had had enough of pity over the last two years. He didn't want to just move into the house like a squatter or a deadbeat son. After all the work he'd put in to build himself into a respectable man, a handout was the last thing he wanted. To that end, he'd hired a realtor to represent his interests in buying the property anonymously. With the money he'd saved up, he had enough for a decent down payment and a year's worth of mortgage payments. Just this morning, he'd gotten a text from the realtor that it was looking good; the house was almost certainly his.

Thus, the lunch break surprise.

It'd been an awfully hard secret to keep. But the look on Rose's face in this moment was absolutely worth it. She looked like she didn't know what to do with her hands. As he gave her the rundown on everything, she kept touching his wrist, her jaw, the window, like she thought she could reach out and pluck the house off the ground herself to give it a squealing hug.

Finally, she took a deep breath, steadied her nerves, and looked at him with an enigmatic smile on her face. Her honey-colored eyes were swimming with a complex mix of emotions. "I can't believe you did this," she said. He could tell that she wanted to say more but didn't quite know how to put it in words. That was fine with him. That smile was all he needed to be certain that he was doing the right thing.

"I did it for us," he said. "I wanted us to have a place to call our own. Is that ... is that okay with you?"

"Oh, Brent!" Her only answer was to grab his face in both hands and kiss him like her life depended on it. She broke away reluctantly and looked down at her wristwatch. "I could sit here and cry for hours, but I have to be back in the classroom in two and a half minutes."

He smiled and turned the keys in the ignition once again. "Say no more," he told her. "This was all I wanted to see."

Brent was still buzzing by the time Rose got home from school later that evening. He'd let himself into her house and was just getting started cooking dinner for the three of them. Susanna came bursting through the door ahead of her mother and went bounding straight up to Henrietta. The two of them had become best friends over the last year. Normally, Henrietta would've been just as excited to see Susanna as Susanna was to see her. But tonight, Henrietta shied away from Susanna's embrace and retreated into a corner with a whine that Brent had never heard her make before.

"That's weird," he muttered to himself, looking at her quizzically.

In all the time he'd had her, Henrietta had always been friendly and playful with just about everybody, especially Susanna. It was highly unlike her to run away from contact instead of seeking it out. Come to think of it, she'd been weird for a few weeks now. Not eating as much, giving up sooner on their morning runs. Maybe she was sick. He oughta take her to the vet soon just to get things checked out.

"Hi, babe," Rose said as she set her stuff down and came in. "What're you doing?"

"Gonna whip us up some dinner." His mind was still on Henrietta, who had now slunk away down the hallway.

"Did you forget?"

"Forget what?"

"We've got dinner at your mom's tonight, space cadet." She tapped him on the forehead. "Remember?"

"Oh!" Brent slapped himself upside the head. "That totally slipped my mind, actually. Welp, guess this will be leftovers." He scraped the stuff he'd started prepping into a Tupperware container and tucked it away in the refrigerator.

Rose laughed. "I'm just gonna freshen up and change real quick, and then we can go."

"Sounds good." He looked over to where Henrietta had gone. "Think we should leave Henrietta here?" he called to Rose as she went to the bedroom in the back. "She's been acting kinda strange lately."

"Really?" came Rose's voice floating down the hall. "I haven't noticed anything."

"Let's just leave her," he decided. "Maybe she just wants some space."

"Whatever you think is best, babe." Rose reemerged a minute later wearing blue jeans and a flowing white blouse. "Ready to go?"

"Yep. Suz, you ready?"

"Yep!" The little girl bounced over from the corner where she kept all her toys, smiling. Rose and Brent each took one of her hands, and together, their little family headed out for dinner at Mom's.

8

ELIZA

"Only five days left, Oliver," Sara teased as she poured herself a glass of chardonnay. "Getting cold feet yet?"

"Not if he knows what's good for him," Eliza cut in with a joking smile.

Oliver raised his hands, pleading his innocence. "Of course not. No cold feet." When Eliza nodded, satisfied with his answer, he leaned over to Rose, who was sitting next to him at the inn's big dinner table, and fake-whispered, "Besides, these Bensons are crazy. She'd hunt me down in no time."

Rose choked on a bite of carrot she'd been halfway to swallowing. Brent, seated on her other side, patted her on the back as she spluttered and rushed to get a sip of water from her glass.

Dinner at the inn tonight had been fun. It was just another Tuesday night, but there was a vibe in the air that this was a special one. Eliza hadn't ever considered herself super religious—though she'd done Sunday school growing up, had her first communion, all that jazz. But in this moment, she had a sudden flashback to something she'd learned way back then: the primary requirement to make a space holy was to have enough people gathered together with love in their hearts.

That's how it felt to have her whole family and all their loved ones here. It felt *sacred.*

"Speaking of the wedding, here comes the future monster-in-law," Holly added with a grin as Mom came swooping into the room with a massive pot full of steaming corn on the cob.

She sat it down with a thunk in the middle of the table, took off her oven mitts, and promptly used one to swat Holly on the top of the head. "Mind your manners, young lady," Mom scolded, biting back a smile of her own. "Your own husband will tell you that I am nothing if not loving to all my children's spouses."

Pete, who already had a mouthful of corn on the cob, nodded fervently. He looked like a kid who'd been asleep at his desk in the back of the room when the teacher called on him to answer a question.

Holly rolled her eyes.

"Like I said, nothing if not loving." Mom turned to go back to the kitchen to retrieve the chicken she'd been baking.

"She's not all sugar and spice, you know." Eliza chuckled. "But she sure is good at acting like it."

"I heard that!" called Mom over her shoulder as she retreated into the kitchen. Her disembodied voice floated around the corner as she added, "And just because it's the week of your wedding doesn't mean I won't give you a swat over the head, too!"

"Thirty-six years old and my mom is still threatening me with physical violence." Eliza groaned. "I thought I would've grown out of that by now."

"Be nice to your momma," Oliver chided. "She cooked us up a serious spread tonight."

That, at least, was inarguable. The table was straining under the weight of carrots, green beans, corn on the cob, chicken, sausage, shrimp, mashed potatoes, baked potatoes, three different kinds of pie, and several bottles of wine. Most of the adults—with the exception of Brent, who was going on almost two years sober—had already polished off a glass or two of vino. Eliza had barely touched hers, though. She was feeling a little nauseous. Something about the wine and the smell was unsettling her stomach a bit, so she decided not to drink too much.

Just then, Marshall Cook came bursting through the front door, arms spread wide like a hometown hero returning from war. He had the biggest, goofiest smile Eliza had ever seen on his face. Which, to be fair, was pretty much par for the course. In all the years that he and Brent had been best buddies, Eliza could count on two fingers the number of times she'd seen Marshall without his trademark mega-watt grin.

"Family, I'm home!" His voice, like always, had a tinge of laughter at the edges, as though he might start guffawing at a moment's notice. It was hard not to smile when he was around.

"Who invited him?" Brent groaned, burying his face in his hands.

"Hey, Marsh," Rose said, waving.

"Well, well, well, who all do we have here?" he boomed.

Everyone else offered hellos and how are yous as Marshall walked around the table shaking hands and kissing cheeks like a politician running for office. He was also not-so-sneakily sampling every one of the dishes on display.

As he moved around the table, he rattled off nicknames like a dad-joke machine gun. Everybody received one upon first meeting Marshall. They were inevitably horrible and inevitably permanent.

"Hemingway! Dinosara! Mojo JoJo! Party Pete! Showstopper! Frizzy Lizzy! Big Slick! Roosevelt! Triple B!"

Everyone followed Brent's lead in groaning and rolling their eyes. Marshall couldn't have cared less. When his circuit was completed, he pulled up a chair, sat down, and started filling up a plate of food at once. "Oh man, this all looks incredible."

"Marshall Cook, where's the love for me?" Mom scolded as she reemerged from the kitchen once more.

Marshall leapt up at once and embraced her, planting a sloppy kiss on her cheek. "Momma Bear!" he crowed. "You know I could never forget you." He took his seat again, still grinning from ear to ear, and resumed loading up his plate. "Where are the little gremlins?" he asked, looking around for the children.

"Well," Eliza answered with a bemused smile as she rose to her feet, "Winter *was* sleeping, and I believe Susanna was quietly coloring. But I have a feeling your grand entrance might've stirred the pot a little bit."

Sure enough, when Eliza got up to check on the pack 'n' play crib where Winter had been peacefully snoozing, she found her daughter wide awake. Susanna was standing on her tiptoes, peering over the edge.

"Is the baby awake?" Susanna asked Eliza.

"Looks like she is." She scooped up Winter, who was still batting sleep out of her eyes, and offered her hand to Susanna. "C'mon, hon," she added, "it's time to eat anyway."

They went back over and settled into their seats. Eliza started spooning mashed potatoes onto a plate to feed Winter. Marshall was mid-story, but she was only half listening.

"... So I'm checking out the radars this morning, like always—"

"Huge weather nerd," Brent interrupted by way of explanation.

"It's called *meteorology*, you peasant," Marshall corrected, lobbing a bread roll at Brent's head, "and as I was saying before I was so rudely cut off, I'm checking the charts and *boom,* my prediction comes true! Huge system pops up out of nowhere. Well, not nowhere. If you know where to look for this stuff ..."

Weather talk couldn't be more boring to Eliza. She tuned out as Winter missed her mouth with the spoon—she was insisting on trying to feed herself these days, with decidedly mixed results—and dropped a huge dollop of mashed potatoes and gravy onto Eliza's leg. As she was cleaning off her jeans, though, something Marshall was saying caught her ear.

"... Could even be an early hurricane by the time it gets here on Saturday."

Eliza froze, then whirled around to face Marshall's end of the table. "What'd you just say?"

He looked at her quizzically with a mouthful of food. "Which part?"

"A hurricane? Here? On Saturday?"

He nodded slowly. "Yeah. Maybe. Still pretty far out; hard to tell. But looks likelier than not."

The color drained from Eliza's face. Everyone else had gone stock-still, too, with the exception of Marshall, who had swallowed one bite of food and launched back into a new tangent of his monologue. It took him a few long beats before he realized that the entire table was frozen.

He looked up and looked around. "What's happening?"

No one answered until Pete finally decided he'd be the one to bite the bullet. "Eliza's wedding is on Saturday," he said quietly.

Marshall's jaw fell open. "Oh no," was all he could muster. "I shouldn't have said anything."

"No, no, it's not your fault," Eliza murmured. But in her head, all she could see was rain lashing at her wedding dress, lightning igniting the floral displays, an angry ocean whipped into a frenzy in the backdrop.

A beach wedding on Nantucket had once seemed like a fantastic idea.

Until, all of a sudden, it didn't.

9

MAE

Marshall's announcement had certainly put a damper on things. That was a crying shame, too, because it had been such a lovely dinner up until then. To her credit, Eliza had done the best she could at bucking up and putting on a smile. Everyone else based their reactions off hers. But Mae knew darn well that her eldest was crushed by the prospect of a storm ruining her wedding day.

And who wouldn't be? Even Eliza—golden child Eliza, everything-always-works-out-for-her Eliza—would be devastated by something like that.

So, though she put on a stiff upper lip and faked it, Mae saw right through her façade. But Eliza didn't want to be comforted. She wanted to go home and cry on Oliver's shoulder, no doubt. Mae noticed how tightly she was squeezing her fiancé's hand under the table. She had hardly touched her wine, either, which was a little out of character for her. All added up, it broke Mae's heart. She had all the faith in the world that things would work out exactly as they were meant to, but she still didn't want to see her firstborn daughter so heartbroken.

The kids had all cleared out in quick fashion as soon as the food was gone and the dishes cleaned up. Mae had insisted that she'd do things herself—"it's really no bother; I like doing dishes!" she'd protested, like she always did—but the adults had waved her off and sprung to work. Clearing, scrubbing, washing, drying, stacking, storing all the leftovers in the fridge or taking some home for themselves. A blur of activity that hardly required much in the way of spoken communication between them. Then they'd said their goodbyes, given their mother a quick kiss on the cheek, and gone home.

In the end, she was left standing idly in the middle of the kitchen, wringing a dish towel between her hands and wondering what else might need doing.

She didn't have too long to contemplate, though. Dominic came trudging down the stairs. She frowned when he rounded the corner and she saw his face. He had a stormy look in his eyes. She glanced down and saw that he had his cell phone in his hand with words on the screen. That in itself was unusual. Dominic was a well-known hater of text messaging. As a matter of fact, he was a vocal critic of the entire telecommunications industry. "They're destroying the King's English!" he'd say bitterly if she caught him when he was a few whiskeys deep and his writing had gone poorly that day. "All the LOLs and TTYLs and LMAOs are bringing about the ruin of the most beautiful language mankind ever devised." Mae would just laugh and roll her eyes.

He stopped in the doorway of the kitchen, phone squeezed tightly in his hand. Mae tapped her foot and waited for him to explain what was going on. He'd been quiet all through dinner. That, too, was unusual. Dominic was a quiet man by nature, but he warmed up as he got to know people. So to hear him not utter a peep the whole meal had triggered the first of the alarm bells in her brain.

This here was number two.

"Well?" Mae asked, hands on her hips. "Are you going to keep me in the dark? Or shall we play a guessing game? I was never very fond of charades, I'm afraid."

He didn't laugh. The smile faded from her face.

"Dom, honey?" she continued. "Is everything all right?"

He didn't look up, but when he spoke, it was in a strange, strangled voice she'd never heard from him before. "I just got a text message," he said, nodding towards his phone. He started to say something else, but fell quiet again before the words got out.

"And ...?" Mae prompted.

He looked up at her finally. His eyes were swimming with a baffling mix of emotions. She usually had a fairly good read on how he was feeling. He was reserved, yes, but after two years under her roof, she was typically pretty spot-on with reading the Dominic signs.

Now, though, she hadn't the faintest idea what was running through his mind.

"It seems ..." he said, clearing his throat. "It seems as though my ex-wife is coming to visit."

The towel Mae was holding fell from her hands. It took every ounce of willpower not to stop her jaw from dropping, too.

"Your ... your ex-wife," she finally managed to say, "is coming. Coming here?"

He nodded.

Now, it was Mae's turn to drown in a baffling mix of emotions. One thought stood out in stark relief above all the others: "You never told me you were married before, Dominic."

His face was clouded over. Was it embarrassment? Shame? What else hadn't he told her?

"I was."

"For how long?"

"Seven years."

"When was this?"

"Long before I came here, I assure you."

Mae honestly didn't know what to think. The first and most startling blow was to think that there were secrets in his past he had kept from her. A marriage was an awfully important life event not to even mention it once in two years of living together. It wasn't that she was mad at him for being married before. She herself had been married, of course. But she certainly hadn't concealed that fact, for crying out loud! Why wouldn't Dominic tell her such a thing?

The existence of an ex-wife was going to take her a long time to brood over. That much was already apparent.

The more immediate and pressing concern was the fact that this mystery woman was going to be coming *here*.

"When is she arriving, Dominic?"

He swallowed hard. Mae watched his Adam's apple rise up and down. "Tomorrow."

That was perhaps the biggest shock of all.

Her boyfriend had an ex-wife, who was coming to visit them unexpectedly.

Tomorrow.

Four days before her daughter's wedding.

"Please tell me you are joking, Dominic."

He shook his head and said nothing else.

"This week, of all weeks."

"I'm sorry," he whispered.

She had never seen him look so defeated before. If she didn't feel anger boiling up deep within her, she might actually feel pity for him. He was normally such a proud, dignified man. A quiet strength exuded from him all the time.

Now, he looked like he wanted to retreat within himself and never come back out.

She didn't have much capacity for pity at the moment, though. She felt more like she'd been slapped in the face.

He had lied to her. A lie by omission, but a lie nonetheless. That had to mean that there were other lies swimming below the surface, just waiting to be dragged up into the light. Mae gripped the edge of the kitchen counter to steady herself. Her head was swimming. She didn't quite trust her balance all of a sudden. It didn't need to be said that she didn't quite trust the man in her kitchen all of a sudden, either.

"I'm sorry," Dominic said again. Then he turned and walked away before she could find the words she wanted to say, shuffling back up the stairs in his house slippers.

Mae stood in the sparkling clean kitchen for a long time. Just an hour ago, this place had been full of life and laughter and love. Now, it felt like the lowest point on earth. She didn't know what to do or say or think.

And she didn't have much time to figure those things out.

Because this woman was coming tomorrow. Was she intending to stay with them? Would she be expecting to attend Eliza's wedding? What was she like? Where was she from? What was her name?

What was her name?

That, of all the billions of questions percolating in Mae's head right now, felt for some bizarre reason like the most important one of all of them.

What was her name?

She wondered what kind of woman a younger Dominic would have swooned over. "Mae" was a simple, honest name. But those traits didn't seem to match the expression that had been marring Dominic's face when he broke the news to her. One did not harbor such fear for a "Mae."

So it was something more exotic then. A "Priscilla," maybe? No, too fussy. A "Florence"? That didn't feel right either.

What about an "Estelle"? That seemed classy, opaque, with an undercurrent of mystery to it. Yes, Mae decided, she would be opening her home tomorrow morning to a woman named Estelle. She could just hear Dominic pronouncing those syllables with his rippling accent. Estelle would be tall, no doubt, verging on Amazonian. Or maybe short? Petite? Would she be blonde or brunette, redheaded or raven-haired? Busty, thin? Friendly, cold? A million possibilities swirled around in Mae's imagination, every single one of them worse than the last.

Jealousy stabbed through her like a lightning bolt. She had that same befuddled feeling she'd had the other day when she was reminiscing on how strange it felt to call Dominic her "boyfriend." Jealousy was a problem she'd left behind almost half a century ago. Or so she thought. But now it was back, and back with a vengeance for having been so long neglected. It was an ugly feeling. Mae wanted badly for it to go away.

She thought of calling Debra or Lola to vent, then thought better of it.

For now, she wanted to lie down in the darkness and brood. "Estelle" was coming tomorrow. Mae needed to get her thoughts in order.

PART II

A GUEST ARRIVES

10

HOLLY

Wednesday morning.
Four days until Eliza's wedding.

Holly woke up on Wednesday like a little kid on Christmas morning. She was out of bed about three seconds after her eyes opened. By the time four or five minutes had passed, she was downstairs—dressed, makeup on, hair and teeth brushed—and putting on breakfast for everybody. Waffles for the kids, eggs and bacon for Pete, coffee and a bagel for her. She was whistling as she cooked.

There was one big, big reason she was so excited: today, the first batch of furniture for Goodwin & Payne Law Firm was due to arrive.

She'd made quick work of the ordering as soon as Pete had given her the go-ahead on Monday. As a matter of fact, she'd stayed up late into the night, finalizing her ideas and placing the initial orders. The truth was that she'd had rough sketches penciled into her notebook for months now, ever since Pete had first broached the possibility of handing the project over to Holly. So it had taken her no time at all to get all her ducks in a row. And since the first order had been placed with a local Nantucket furniture company, it was only a one-day turnaround on the shipping. Light-speed. Holly couldn't be more thrilled.

She wanted to *touch* something, to put a project together with her own two hands. Raising her children as a stay-at-home mom felt both slower and less tangible than she might've thought. Sure, there was plenty of day-to-day work that required her getting her own hands dirty. Laundry, cooking, cleaning, helping out with homework —the list never ended, really. Those things were all satisfying in their own way. No one loved a clean house more than Holly Goodwin.

But it wasn't the same as turning an empty space into something beautiful. Moving into the new house had scratched some of that itch, though the manner in which the whole house-theft thing went down had poisoned it somewhat. This, however, was a fresh opportunity. Clean slate. From nothing to something.

She couldn't wait.

Pete lumbered downstairs a few minutes after her. "Good morning, sweetheart!" she beamed, pecking him on the cheek when he passed by.

He scratched his head and smiled. "Someone's up and at 'em today."

"Why wouldn't I be? It's another day in paradise with you, my love."

Pete shot her a sideways glance as he poured himself a cup of coffee from the French press. "And yet, I'm worried. Should I be worried? You're worrying me."

The waffles popped out of the toaster. Holly was quick to plate them and set them in the kids' places at the breakfast bar. "The only thing you need to be worried about is how much I love you, darling."

He chuckled as he took a sip and immediately winced. Pete *hated* hot coffee. Another Pete Thing. "I haven't been worried about that since the day we met, Hollz."

The kids came scampering down before Holly could do anything but smile. They slid onto their stools. Grady immediately started pouring an obscene amount of syrup onto his food, while Alice picked up her fork and knife and began to fastidiously cut her waffles into circles. That was her new thing. Circles tasted better, apparently.

"Grady!" reprimanded Holly. "That is *plenty* of syrup, hon."

He grumbled but set the syrup aside and went to town on the waffles with his bare hands. Holly rolled her eyes and let it go for the time being. She was in too good of a mood to keep lecturing everybody. If Alice wanted circles, let her have circles! If Grady wanted to eat like a caveman, let him do it! It was a beautiful day, the birds were chirping, the sun was shining, and nobody on the planet could do her wrong.

She busied herself with packing the kids' lunches as Pete disappeared back into their bedroom to get dressed for work. She glanced up to check the clock on the microwave as she finished zipping up the lunch boxes and setting them on the entranceway table so the kids could grab them on their way out the door. It was 7:43 in the morning. She had to drop the kids off at school, then be over to the old firehouse by eight-thirty to supervise the furniture delivery and unloading process. Plenty of time. This morning was going swimmingly already.

She thought about Eliza out of nowhere and felt a pang of pity. The bombshell Marshall had dropped last night about the incoming hurricane had really ruined the evening. Holly still had her fingers crossed that it wouldn't be a problem, but Pete had checked on some weather websites last night and agreed with Marshall's assessment. "It looks a little grim, to be honest," he'd said. "Let's hope it works out."

Pete reemerged in his suit and tie.

"Look at my dashing husband," Holly exclaimed giddily, with just a touch of over-the-top melodrama, because it always made Pete smile. She grabbed him by the lapels of his suit jacket and smooched him on the lips. Behind her, Grady and Alice made gagging noises.

Pete's eyes were twinkling as they separated. "Now I'm *definitely* worried," he commented. "You going to be okay today, bossing around all those moving men?"

"I was born to do this," she answered at once.

He laughed again. "That I believe," he said. He checked his wristwatch. "All right, I gotta scoot. We've got clients coming in at 8:15. Text me and let me know how everything goes?"

"Will do, honey."

He kissed her again, gave each of the kids a kiss of their own on the top of the head, then went out the door.

Holly made short work of the kids' plates and cutlery as they went to finish getting ready for the school day. Summer break was in the very near future. She could sense that they were already antsy to be free of their teachers. They were both excited to go to their respective summer camps, too. Holly had found a science program for Grady that looked great, primarily because it involved blowing things up. Alice would be going to a ballet "boot camp" with a couple of her friends from dance class. Holly thought that sounded a little intense for a seven-year-old, but it seemed to be all the rage, so she just shrugged it off.

By 7:58, they were all loaded up into the minivan and pulling out of the driveway. Holly clicked on the radio and sang under her breath to an old Shania Twain song as they made their way across the island and into the car drop-off line at Nantucket Elementary.

"Bye, honeys!" she said when she dropped them off. Alice waved back, Grady grunted something that vaguely resembled a goodbye, and then the door clicked shut and they were gone.

Furniture time!

As Holly drove over to the future home of Goodwin & Payne, drumming her fingers on the steering wheel to the tune, she wondered for a minute if she was being silly. It was just furniture, after all. Surely she had more important things in her life to get excited about.

Well, yes, that might be true, but who cared? Let her get excited about this! Enthusiasm was in such short supply in the world these days. It was better to let people like what they liked. Holly liked furniture, she liked decorating, she liked pretty things and neat spaces. If that made her happy, then so be it.

When she was about thirty seconds away from her destination, she realized suddenly that she had left the keys to the building at home. "Shoot!" she said, slapping herself in the forehead. What a dumb mistake. She thought about just turning around, but she thought she spied the corner of the delivery truck sticking out around the corner. She'd just pop in and let them know she had to run back real quick.

She pulled around and saw that the delivery was in fact there already, ahead of schedule. The two uniformed men were leaning against the hood of the truck. She waved at them.

"Hi!" she hollered out of her open window. "I'm so sorry, but I forgot the keys at home. It'll be just a sec; I'm going to grab them right now."

"No worries, ma'am," the taller one replied with a friendly smile. "If it's all right with you, we'll just start getting the stuff off the truck, then?"

She gave him a thumbs-up and a "Go for it!" Then she turned the car around and headed back home. It was 8:12 now according to the car clock, and it would take her at least ten minutes each way. Oh well, nothing she could about it. They seemed like nice men.

Two Fleetwood Mac songs later, she pulled up in the driveway at home and ran inside to retrieve the keys. Then she was back on the road, singing louder now.

But when she arrived back at the firehouse, what she saw there didn't make any sense.

The delivery men were putting the furniture *back* onto the truck. What on earth? Holly parked, frowning, and got out of the corner. "Hello ..." she called. "I'm sorry, has there been some mistake?"

The tall delivery man she'd spoken to just a few minutes ago set down a heavy filing cabinet with an *oomph* and wiped his hands on his pants. He jerked a thumb over his shoulder, towards the other side of the moving truck.

"You'll have to talk to her," he explained apologetically. "We had most of the stuff off, and she came storming up and told us to put everything back on right away. Seemed real irate about the whole thing." He shrugged. "Guess you ladies oughta figure it out?"

Holly's stomach dropped.

She knew, without even having to think about it, who was on the other side of the truck. Slowly, her feet carried her around the back of the car. She weaved through the furniture she'd picked out, the furniture she loved, the furniture she'd woken up thinking about with a huge smile on her face, as each piece awaited its turn to be loaded back up and returned to where it had come from.

There was no smile as she walked around and saw Cecilia Payne standing there with her arms crossed over her chest.

Cecilia was scowling viciously as she berated the second delivery man. "... don't know on *whose* authority you brought this *junk* ..." When she heard Holly approaching, her gaze swiveled around and her scowl deepened. Holly stood still like she'd been frozen in place, skewered there by Cecilia's glare.

The woman started in at once. "I am sorry," she began, though she didn't sound sorry in the slightest, "but this just will not do. These selections look absolutely horrific. Shoddily made, and the selection is dreadful, to say the least. I will not have my husband represented by such hideous decor. It's all going back at once to whatever swamp you found it in. And," she added, "I'll be taking over the interior design responsibilities. You clearly have no aptitude for it."

Holly opened her mouth, then shut it again. She couldn't think. She couldn't speak. This was all just a bad nightmare, right? Surely no one could be so cruel to another person, especially not right to her face. Their husbands worked together, for goodness' sake! Holly knew that she and Cecilia were never going to be best friends, but still ... this was a bridge too far.

More than anything, she wanted to cry. But that was the one thing she refused to do. Not in front of this witch. She wouldn't dare give Cecilia the satisfaction of seeing her shed a tear.

Retreating felt awful. It felt cowardly. But if she didn't distance herself right now, she was going to absolutely crumble to pieces. She needed distance, STAT. So, without saying a word, Holly turned tail and fled.

She felt Cecilia's eyes on her as she ran away.

Holly drove straight to Pete's temporary office at his friend Ethan's real estate firm. She didn't say hello to the secretary as she stormed in, still biting back tears. Nor did she say a single word to Billy when she threw open the door of the conference room they were camping out in. Pete looked up and knew at once that something was wrong.

"Be right back," he muttered to Billy. Then he got up and led Holly back outside. They climbed back into her car. Only then did she let loose the tears that she'd been holding back since the moment she first saw Cecilia Payne.

She boohoo-cried like a little girl for three or four long minutes. Pete —her beautiful, kind, blissfully ignorant husband—just stroked her hair and let her cry. Eventually, she sniffled and pulled herself together.

This was not over.

She explained in a low voice what had happened. When she relayed Cecilia's words, Pete's eyes widened.

"She didn't ... she couldn't have ... I mean, she wouldn't ..." he sputtered.

But he knew well that she could, she would, she had. He'd met her. He saw the best in everyone—that was one of his best qualities—but even the eternally cheery Pete Goodwin knew that Cecilia had a deep reservoir of nastiness in her.

"What do you want to do?" he settled on finally. "I could talk to Billy—"

"No," Holly said, cutting him off with a sudden firmness. She felt embarrassed—not for running from Cecilia or crying in front of Pete, but for crying instead of doing what she should have done, which was get *angry*. She should have stood her ground. She should have said something. Anything. Fought back. Holly Benson Goodwin was neither a quitter nor a coward.

"Are you sure?" Pete asked, eyeing her.

"Yes," she answered at once. She squeezed the steering wheel with both hands until her knuckles went white. The urge to keep crying had vanished as suddenly as it had come. In its place was roiling anger. She was going to go back to the firehouse, she was going to find Cecilia Payne, and she was going to speak her mind to her.

"Final answer?" Pete asked one more time, just to be sure.

Holly looked over at him. "Final answer," she said. "I'm going to handle this myself."

11

MAE

Mae hadn't slept a wink the night before. Dominic, no doubt sensing that Mae was not in the least happy with him, had spent the night in the armchair downstairs. He did that from time to time, usually when he was staying up late reading, or if he passed out in a torpor after writing until the early hours of the morning. Mae had gotten used to going to bed without him. A night owl, she was not.

Usually, though, he came to bed sometime in the middle of the night. She slept better when she could sense him breathing next to her. But last night, he didn't come up.

Dominic hadn't said when his ex-wife would be arriving. Mae couldn't decide if she wanted to ask him or not, either. On one hand, waiting on pins and needles for an unspecified arrival was no fun at all. But staring at the second hand winding away on the grandfather clock downstairs wasn't much better.

She decided not to ask him. Or even to say a word to him. Instead, she busied herself with as many tiny chores around the house as she could dream up. Without guests to keep mucking things around, she finally had an opportunity to get some true deep cleaning done.

She scrubbed the gunk built up on the showerheads and faucets with an old toothbrush, wiped down the blades of the ceiling fans, and replaced each of the air filters in the guest rooms. She went through both the kitchen refrigerator and the spare they kept in the garage to throw out those items that snuck away to the back of the freezer and seemed to linger there forever. She ran the dishwasher with a cup of vinegar, passed a rag and cleaning solution over every reflective surface she could find, and put each of the shower curtains through a wash cycle.

The cleaning was a good distraction while it lasted. She did her best to keep her mind focused on the task at hand. For the most part, she was successful.

But when she was all done, maybe-Estelle-maybe-not had still not arrived. So Mae took a shower, blew out her hair, applied a light touch of makeup, and got dressed in a light red summer dress.

Stepping in front of the full-length mirror in the innkeeper's bedroom, she checked over her appearance. Sixty-two sounded quite a bit older than she felt, she decided. If she closed her eyes, she felt much the same as she did when she was twenty-six. She wasn't about to be put out to pasture, or swept away into irrelevance by her boyfriend's ex-wife.

"No," she said out loud. It felt good to say. "No."

When she opened her eyes again, she smiled at her reflection. She felt good—or rather, she decided that she was going to feel good, despite the situation at hand. Maybe-Estelle was coming into *her* home, after all. She ought not feel so dismayed.

Then the doorbell dinged.

Mae froze, waiting with bated breath. She heard Dominic open the door and then a woman say, in a lilting Irish accent, "Well, it's quite a bit smaller than I'd anticipated!"

Oh, today was going to be a bad day.

"Hello, Saoirse," Dominic said. His voice was quiet but clear.

"Saoirse," Mae repeated to herself under her breath in the bedroom upstairs. Not Estelle, but Saoirse. "*Seer-shuh.* Saoirse." The name felt clumsy coming out of Mae's mouth, whereas it had such a pleasing bounce when Dominic said it.

The time had come for Mae to go downstairs. Despite the forced-upon-her circumstances of the whole thing, Saoirse was in fact her guest. Hospitality was in Mae's bones.

She let out a long, rattling sigh, then made her way down the staircase.

She held her breath as she rounded the corner. Three more steps. Two more. One more ...

Then, she was in the spotlight.

Dominic and Saoirse looked at her. She paused for the briefest of seconds to take in the scene.

Dominic looked fidgety. He was wearing his favorite cardigan, Mae noticed with mild irritation. A soft blue one, over a white button-down shirt. And he'd put on real shoes, proper leather loafers, instead of his normal house slippers. That irked her, too.

Standing to his right was formerly-known-as-maybe-Estelle, now revealed as Saoirse. She looked quite a bit like an old British actress that Mae's mother had loved named Amanda Redman. She had a broad smile that thinned her blue eyes out, high cheekbones, and blonde hair with a reddish tint that fell in gentle curls down past her shoulders. She was just about Mae's height, though the high heels she was wearing elevated her a touch more. She'd chosen a pale pink dress that was flattering to her complexion. It looked quite nice next to Dominic's robin's egg blue cardigan, actually.

Mae noticed in quick succession that Dominic had already taken Saoirse's bag from her—an expensive leather duffle with a designer logo emblazoned across it—and that Saoirse's hand rested lightly on Dominic's forearm.

"Hello," Mae said, forcing herself to walk forward and offer her hand to shake. "I'm Mae."

"Saoirse," the woman replied, her smile fading a touch. "I've heard much about you." Her handshake was soft and limp, almost like a member of royalty who half expected you to kiss the back of her knuckles.

"Have you now?" Mae answered. "Why, I wish I could say the same. But Dominic here has been rather tight-lipped about you, dear! Isn't that so?"

She glared at Dominic to punctuate the jab. But she immediately felt guilty for doing so. She was mad, yes, for many valid reasons, but this kind of catty subterfuge wasn't like her at all.

In a vacuum, there was nothing outwardly wrong or offensive about Saoirse. She deserved the benefit of the doubt, just like every one of Mae's guests, didn't she? Considering the way they were meeting, maybe the two of them wouldn't ever be the best of pals, but it didn't reflect well on Mae's manners to purposefully throw Saoirse off-balance within moments of her walking in the door. The best course of action would be to treat her politely and hope that her stay at the Sweet Island Inn was a short one.

"Our Dominic is full of surprises, you'll find," Saoirse responded cryptically.

Mae cringed inwardly. *Our* Dominic? It was like nails on a chalkboard. Again, she had that fleeting feeling that she was much too old to be engaged in games like this. But she was in the thick of it, whether she liked it or not.

"That certainly seems to be the case," she murmured.

Dominic, for his part, had hardly said a word since Mae came down the stairs. He looked wildly uncomfortable. Mae didn't feel too bad for him.

"Dominic, darling, why don't you show me to my room?" Saoirse said, though her eyes never left Mae's.

"Of course," he mumbled. "This way." He gestured up the stairs and the two of them went off, leaving Mae standing alone in the foyer.

"And the first thing she says is, '*Well, it's quite a bit smaller than I anticipated!*'" Mae exclaimed. She looked around as soon as the words left her mouth. She hoped that no one else she knew was in the restaurant. She and Debra had sequestered themselves at a corner table at a little cafe downtown. But Nantucket was a small island—someone always knew someone who knew the person you were talking about. Discretion was important.

In this case, though, Mae couldn't care less about courtesy. It felt as though Saoirse had trampled all over her world as soon as she'd crossed the doorway. Less than twenty-four hours ago, Mae didn't even know this woman existed. Now, she was the only thing she could think about.

"She did not," Debra said in disbelief.

"She most certainly did."

Debra sipped her iced tea through a straw. "I honestly cannot believe that. Does she know about you and Dominic?"

Mae shrugged. "Who's to say? I don't know what she does or doesn't know. For crying out loud, I don't even know what *I* don't know! Dominic has never mentioned her even once!"

Her friend tapped her nails on the rim of her glass. "I'd be furious if I were you," she said. "This whole thing is just—well, it's unbelievable, frankly. You'd think a man of his age would know the importance of communication."

"I would've thought so, too," Mae said. Truth be told, she was more sad than mad at this point. Once upon a time, she might've been fiery about the whole situation. Not anymore. It felt like a heavy weight was settling over her heart. She felt betrayed, in a sickening kind of way. Dominic was turning out to be much different than the man she'd thought he was.

Mae tried to keep the focus on him in her mind. He, after all, was the one with whom she had a true and meaningful relationship, not his ex-wife. But, try as she might, her thoughts kept drifting back to Saoirse. She wanted badly to hate the woman. She combed over her in her mind's eye. Those *heels*. That *bag*. Her *handshake*. Any one of those things would be enough to draw Mae's ire. All together, they added up to something comically offensive, almost.

It felt wrong to be so mad at this "other woman," when she had no cause to dislike her at all, other than that she had once been romantically involved with Mae's boyfriend. And yet, she couldn't help it. She was mad at Saoirse and yet not mad enough. The same went for Dominic. She just couldn't decide where to direct her energy.

"Eliza deserves better than this," Mae said.

"Mhmm," Debra agreed. "It's rude of this woman to just show up unannounced, don't you think?"

"I suppose," Mae mused. "Though I do wonder how long Dominic has known this might happen."

Debra tilted her head quizzically. "You think he might've kept this from you for a while?"

"It's just so hard to say." Mae sighed and fell silent. She'd hardly touched her salad. Even a little nibble seemed unappetizing. She was sick with worry and sick of feeling that way. Scarcely two hours had passed since Saoirse's arrival and she'd already turned Mae's world upside down. She couldn't wait until this impromptu visit was over.

"Anyway," she said abruptly, straightening up, "I've had quite enough of moaning about my problems for the time being. What's new in your world, love?"

"Oh, not much," Debra answered vacantly. Mae knew that there was something hiding under the surface there. Debra always had to be coaxed into talking about her feelings.

"Don't you be keeping secrets, too!" Mae chided playfully, lightly smacking the back of Debra's hand on the table. "Goodness knows I am dealing with enough of that at the moment."

Debra smiled. "All right, all right, that's reasonable. I'm just ..." She looked up at Mae, who was astonished to see the glimmer of a tear in her friend's eye. "I'm just lonely, Mae."

"Oh, honey." She laced her fingers through Debra's and squeezed to reassure her friend. "I know just how you feel."

"I know you do. That's why I'm okay with talking to you about it. I just —oh, I don't know. I don't want to say I 'need a man' in my life, because that feels so vapid and silly. But I miss having that partner, you know? A companion."

Mae nodded as Debra talked about how it felt to come back to her empty apartment each night. She kept busy during the day in much the same way Mae had done before the inn came around— volunteering, exercising, visiting with friends, participating in her church and her book club. But at the end of the day, when the lights were off and she was in bed, she was alone. That could be such a challenging burden to bear. The silence, Mae knew, was so oppressive sometimes.

"Have you thought about looking for someone?" Mae asked.

Debra laughed hollowly. "Where would I do that?"

"You could try online dating," she suggested.

"Hmm. That's an interesting idea. I don't know about all that, though. It just seems so ... well, vulnerable, maybe? You never know who's who on the Internet."

"That's true—or at least, it can be, from what I hear. But it seems to be much safer than it once was. There are certainly a lot of people in our position, you know—older and not ready to just give up on life."

"You're right about that, definitely."

"I was just thinking this morning that I may have some wrinkles, but there's a lot of life left in me."

Debra laughed again, but this time there was more cheer and less sorrow in her voice. "You're right about that. My knees disagree sometimes, but my heart is as young as ever. Maybe you're right about the online dating thing, too."

"Worth a browse, certainly. No one said you have to meet up with anyone. But it couldn't hurt to trade messages with someone, right?"

"Right again. Thanks, darling. You're a good friend."

The two women stood up and hugged each other, then walked out of the restaurant arm in arm. They both felt a bit better than they had when they first walked in.

As Debra was driving her back to the inn, Mae heard the weatherman on the radio. "Turn this up!" she yelped.

Debra frowned and cranked up the volume knob just in time to hear him say, "... prospects for a landfall in Nantucket seem to be consolidating on a target date of this Saturday. Residents are advised to prepare for a one- to two-day shelter-in-place warning."

"Oh no," Mae murmured as the radio show went to commercial break. "Poor Eliza."

Debra, too, was shaking her head. "Fingers crossed for her," she said. "I hope that man is wrong. Seems like we're all having a terrible run of bad luck around here."

Mae nodded and looked out the window. It was a beautiful day. Nevertheless, everything was looking awfully grim.

12

SARA

Mom sure seemed glad to have errands to keep her away from the inn. That was weird. Under normal circumstances, Mom was reluctant to leave the inn at all. Sara had even offered to take care of today's tasks another time. Next week, maybe, after all the wedding craziness was done. There was no need to start cleaning out the house on Howard Street right now. Even if this anonymous mystery buyer that Mom mentioned didn't fall through—which Sara was highly skeptical of—there was still plenty of time to get the place all ready for move-in before the closing date arrived.

But Mom insisted. "Let's just get it done!" she'd said brightly in that *Don't ask me again* tone that Sara knew so well.

Sara shrugged. So be it. She was taking the afternoon away from Little Bull to clear her head anyway. It'd be good to have some busywork to keep her mind occupied.

Plus, she liked going back to the house on Howard Street where she had grown up. Even though she and Joey had been living together in their apartment for nearly eight months now, returning to Howard Street always felt like going home. Like going *home* home. It smelled like home. She knew where the creaks in the floors were. She knew which stairs to skip if she was trying to sneak out at night. It just felt good to be under that roof. Like, happy, in the strangest way.

Sara could use a little bit of that right now.

After Hogan's review was published, she'd felt like an imposter in her own world. Walking into Little Bull the next morning was awful, an experience she never, ever wanted to repeat. Even now, months and months later, she hated the sight of herself in the mirror. *Poser,* her reflection seemed to be screaming at her. *Failure.* Maybe a nice, sunny afternoon of listening to music and cleaning out the closets with Mom would be just what the doctor called for.

When they got there, they threw open all the windows and set all the fans on high to circulate that sweet Nantucket breeze throughout the house. Mom put a record on the old record player downstairs and they got to work. They started on the ground floor, organizing what remained in the house into neat, labeled boxes. Most of it was going to be either donated or put into a storage unit that Eliza had gotten for the items Mom couldn't yet bear to part with.

Bit by bit, they deconstructed Sara's childhood and packed it all away. It was equal parts cathartic and hilarious. They'd done this in stages over the last two years, ever since Mom moved into the Sweet Island Inn and began toying with the idea of selling the house, so the stuff that still needed sorting was often the randomest-seeming junk. Eliza's softball mitts, old fishing lures of Brent's, dolls that a young Holly had loved and lost. Sara found an old dress of her mother's that was nearly twice as old as Sara. She held it over her clothes and danced around the room, singing old Disney tunes, while Mom laughed. "Don't make fun of me," she reprimanded, though she was chuckling. "That was the height of fashion, once upon a time."

"Yeah, in the Ice Age, maybe."

Mom threw a shoe at her in response.

When downstairs had been stripped bare, they moved to the bedrooms on the second floor. Those too had been mostly picked through, with each of the kids taking what they wanted and disposing of what they didn't. They saved Mom and Dad's old bedroom for last. There was a little bit of a strange atmosphere hanging over that end of the hallway. Like a little bit of Dad might still be circulating in the air, mixed in with the motes of dust. By cleaning out the last of their things, it felt like cleaning him out, too.

The truth was that it was time for this to happen. A little overdue, in fact. Mom didn't need this house anymore, and though it had been paid off a long time ago, the best move for everybody was to sell it to a new owner and let them create their own memories within its walls. Sara could tell that her mother was sad about it, but only sad in the way that an adult is sad when the time finally comes to give up their favorite childhood stuffed animal. There is no use for it anymore, but it still is so full of memories that your heart will always reach out for it and say, *Well, not quite yet. You can stay just a little bit longer.*

Still, Sara was proud of her mom for taking this step, and she knew her siblings were, too. They'd all been very careful to monitor their mother's emotions, even in the midst of their own respective sorrows and crazy life twists. And Mom had done so well after Dad's accident. She was a worker bee, there was no doubt about that, and she'd found a good man in Dominic when the timing was right for her to open up her heart again.

That being said, however, she was being awfully short on the subject whenever Sara mentioned something in passing about Dominic.

"What's he doing today?" she'd asked when picking up her mother to come over here.

"Oh, I haven't the faintest," Mom had answered. She changed the subject quickly.

Sara frowned, then shrugged and kept working through the depths of her father's old closet. If they were having a tiff, she was sure that both of them were grown enough to settle it on their own. She wouldn't pry too much.

"Well, would you look at this!" her mother said suddenly from the other corner of the closet. She was holding something in her hands, but Sara couldn't see it from where she was. Groaning, she took to her feet and walked over to take a look.

Lying in the middle of her mother's cupped palms was a chunk of wood. As Sara knelt over, she saw that it was a half-finished carving. The back half was still squared off and raw, but the front half had been whittled into a rearing bull. Eyes narrowed, nostrils flared, a ring in its nose that looked so lifelike she could swear it was swinging back and forth with each imaginary pawing of the animal's hoof on the dirt of a bullfighters' arena.

"I believe this was for you," Mom said softly. She handed the carving over.

Sara took it with fingers that were suddenly trembling. She turned around and went to sit on the bed. The mattress wheezed under her weight, spewing dust into the air, but Sara was the one who felt like she'd been hit.

Mom was right; this was definitely intended for her. *My little bull,* her father had always called her whenever she got worked up and was having trouble calming down. That temper had faded a little bit over the years. Actually, now that Sara thought about it, it had faded a lot. She was born to be a brawler, but enduring hardship upon hardship had tamped down her fighting spirit. It felt like there wasn't much of it left these days.

She thought about how she'd spent last night, and the night before, and the night before that, and a long, unbroken chain of nights stretching back twelve months: reading that stupid, spiteful review. Doing it was like sandpapering down her soul, and yet she did it anyway. Punishing herself for standing up for her own dignity.

This bull was like a reminder of her own strength. It was the namesake of her restaurant. But somehow, she'd forgotten what it meant to her. *Little bull.* Those words were her father telling her who she was deep inside.

Screw Gavin Crawford. Screw Martin Hogan. Their opinions didn't matter in the slightest. She had her father's love, and her mother's, and her sisters', and her brother's, and Joey's, and her staff's, and her clients', and—perhaps most importantly of all—her own. That was an important thing to remember.

Now, she had her father's carving to remind her.

She looked up at her mom. "Thanks, Momma," she whispered. "I needed this."

13
HOLLY

Holly spent the rest of the day brooding.

Her brain was spilling over with all the things she wanted to say to Cecilia Payne. And not just say—she wanted to stand on top of a mountain and announce them through the world's loudest megaphone. She wanted to stomp her feet and tear her hair out and scream until she was blue in the face. Cecilia deserved no less than Holly's peak rage. How *dare* she be so rude?

It had been a year of subtle, almost unnoticeable micro-aggressions. But this was the big culmination. After this, there was no going back. Holly knew full well that she might be making her husband's life a little more awkward at work, but she could not care less. Cecilia had crossed the line. Holly was about to kick her butt right back over it.

It was time to go speak her mind.

Cecilia wasn't at the firehouse when Holly pulled up around sunset, minivan tires screeching. The place was empty, with the furniture truck having long since been sent back to its origin, still bearing the cargo Holly had been so excited about.

No matter. Holly was intent on hunting Cecilia to the ends of the earth if that's what it took. She wasn't going to tolerate even a single day more of her disrespect. She'd check her house next.

That thought made Holly even angrier, though she didn't think that was possible. Cecilia's house was stolen property. Holly and Pete had picked it out. Holly and Pete had made an offer. Holly and Pete had been mere days away from closing when an "anonymous someone" had come swooping in with such a sweetheart offer that the seller had reneged, even though they were under contract. It made Holly sick just to think about it. She knew Pete considered all of that ancient history—"water under the bridge," was his exact phrasing whenever the subject came up. But that always enraged her, too.

"It wasn't fair!" she'd snap. "They stole that house!"

"Yeah, I can see how you'd think that," he'd reply.

She still didn't have a good answer for him that didn't involve a few choice words.

The truth was that she and Cecilia had been driving towards this fight since the moment Holly and Pete first made landfall on Nantucket. What she didn't know was whether Cecilia was aware of that, or if she was just that nasty by nature. Holly wasn't quite the same natural optimist that Pete was, but over the years, a little bit of her husband's faith in the goodness of people had rubbed off on her. She wanted to believe that Cecilia didn't harbor evil intentions in her heart around the clock. That sounded exhausting, if nothing else. But all the evidence pointed to the contrary. She was either willfully cruel or blissfully ignorant to just how foul she was capable of being. Holly wasn't sure which was worse.

Rounding the corner, she saw the house at the end of the street. Her heart sagged a little bit at the sight of it. It was still beautiful. That yard was so lush and green, the lines of the roof so sharp and pleasing to the eye.

"Focus," she muttered to herself under her breath. "You've got a job to do."

Holly pulled up in the driveway, wrenched the car into park, and stomped up to the front door. She disregarded the doorbell in favor of hammering on the door with a closed fist. She could see the roof of Cecilia's Range Rover through the window in the garage door, so she knew she was home. The question was, would she answer?

As it turned out, yes.

But the door didn't open to reveal the bristling enemy combatant that Holly had geared herself up to expect. Cecilia stiffened when she saw who was standing on her stoop. She looked less angry than ... afraid? Embarrassed, like she'd been caught doing something wrong? Whatever the emotion was, it put a little hitch in Holly's step. She hesitated and stammered before finally delivering the opening salvo she'd been planning since that morning. "I—uh, I need to talk to you," she said. It came out of her mouth like air leaking out of a balloon.

"Okay," Cecilia responded quietly with a nod. "Would you like to come in?"

Politeness was the last thing Holly had expected, even if it was Cecilia's brand of weirdly formal, uptight politeness, like she'd bought manners from a store and learned how to use them from the instructions that came in the box.

"Um—yes," Holly said defiantly. "I would."

Cecilia stepped aside, holding the door open for her, and Holly entered.

The house smelled different than Holly's. A strong scent of vanilla hung in the air, like Cecilia had just finished baking. That, too, threw Holly off. She had imagined a stench of fire and brimstone following Cecilia around everywhere she went.

Cecilia shut the door behind her and turned to Holly. "Do you want to take a seat at the table?" Her voice was muted and flat. Holly didn't know what to make of that. She didn't know what to make of any of this. All she knew was that her rage was sputtering in her belly, unspent and confused.

"Yes," she mumbled. She followed Cecilia to the dining room table, over which hung a massive and ridiculously expensive-looking chandelier. Both women took a seat, sitting on the edge of their chairs like they might have to leap up at any moment.

"What would you like to talk about?" Cecilia asked.

Holly wasn't ready for that question, or any of the other questions Cecilia had asked thus far.

"I was a little upset by what happened this morning." Holly felt as stiff as Cecilia looked.

"I see."

"I felt that you were rude."

"Mm."

"And condescending."

"Mm."

"And my feelings were hurt."

Cecilia *mm*'d again, and as much as Holly wanted to be mad about that, too, it honestly wasn't a rude *mm*. It was simply the noise you make when someone had a lot to say and you didn't want to interrupt them just yet.

"And ..." Holly was stuck. This sucked! Why couldn't Cecilia have the decency to be the same witch she was this morning? If she did that, at least Holly would feel justified in yelling at her! She tried to summon the memory of their encounter at the firehouse, but it was already fading away in the presence of this new Cecilia seated across from her. This Cecilia was frozen stiff like she was scared and didn't want to make any sudden movements. It was all bizarre and confounding.

"You don't like me, do you?" Cecilia asked suddenly.

Holly nearly did a double take. Her head was reeling. Not one piece of this was unfolding the way she'd had in mind.

So she decided to just speak the truth. "Not really. I don't think you like me, either."

"That's not true," Cecilia answered at once. She was still stiff through her spine, but her face had eased somewhat. Her eyes were glazed over, like she was looking inward. "I don't dislike you at all. I suppose I admire you."

Holly pinched herself to ensure that she wasn't dreaming. "You what?"

"I admire you, I said."

"No, I heard you. What does that mean?"

Cecilia laughed. Honest-to-goodness laughed, like this whole thing was hilarious. Well, to be fair, it wasn't exactly a knee-slapper laugh— more like a hollow, sad, self-deprecating laugh—but it was a laugh nonetheless. "I guess you wouldn't know it from the way I spoke this morning."

"I mean ... can you blame me?"

"No, I don't think I can."

"I would've said that you hated me."

"I can see how you'd think that."

"So ..." Holly noticed suddenly that Cecilia was clenching her hands tightly together to stop them from trembling. "Are you okay?"

Then her gaze went up to Cecilia's face and she saw that the woman was crying.

What. Was. Happening?

"I'm unable to have children," Cecilia blurted at once. The words came pouring out of her like they were desperate to be set free. "I was notified this morning that the final round of IVF was unsuccessful, and the doctor recommended that I not try again. I will never be a mother."

All of a sudden, it was Holly who was lost. "I'm ... I'm sorry?" She frowned and said it again, more like an actual gesture of sympathy than a token offering. "I'm sorry. That is ... that's hard to hear, if it's important to you."

"It is," Cecilia answered. She sniffled. "Or rather, it was, I guess. I don't think it can be important to me anymore from now on."

Holly opened her mouth but there wasn't really anything she could think of to say. She was obviously witnessing a devastating moment in this woman's life. But she barely knew her! Why was Cecilia confessing all this? Up until two minutes ago, Holly was certain that they were sworn enemies. Now, Cecilia was crying in front of her and telling her about these deep-seated desires to be a mother that would never come to fruition. It was enough of an about-face to give her whiplash.

"I'm sorry, Cecilia, but I honestly don't know what to tell you."

Cecilia raised a hand and sniffled once more. A lone tear trickled down her cheek. The gold bracelets on her wrist jangled. "I don't expect you to tell me anything. As I said, I know you don't like me."

"That's not—I don't ..."

"No, it's quite okay. I have treated you poorly. I know that."

Holly was dumbfounded.

Cecilia glanced up from her lap and locked eyes with Holly. "You have a beautiful family. I think I'm just jealous for what you have that I can't."

So that was it. Jealousy for Holly's children. That explained the cruelty, the condescension, the—well, the everything that Cecilia had thrown at Holly since day one. It was sad and bitter and hurtful, and yet it all made sense. Holly felt just as sorry for this broken woman as she had once felt angry towards her.

They sat in silence for a few long minutes while Holly processed everything that was happening. Cecilia sniffled once or twice, but said nothing.

Until, as if some timer had gone off in her head, she stood up. "I don't mean to keep you here listening to me pity myself." There was some of her old royal archness back in her demeanor, though Holly saw— now that she was looking closely—that it seemed to have heartbreak lingering behind it. "I am sorry for what I said this morning. I don't mean to blame my problems on you. I won't stand in your way at the office any longer." She nodded once, as if to herself.

"Oh ... okay," Holly said. "Thanks. Thank you, I mean."

It felt like an unspoken truce was being formed between them. They might not ever be friends, but they had shared a powerful and utterly strange moment at this dining room table, under the light of this magnificent, absurd chandelier. Holly knew that it would take her quite a long time to chew through everything that had happened.

All things considered, it was as satisfying a victory as she was going to get. She said her goodbyes to Cecilia, half wondering if they were going to hug.

But they didn't. Cecilia walked her to the door and Holly went out to her car in a daze.

A year's worth of enmity, swept away without a trace under something so wildly unexpected. She'd gotten what she came for, in a manner of speaking. But it didn't look anything like she once thought she wanted, not so long ago.

14

ELIZA

Wednesday night.

~

It was supposed to be a happy week. It really, really did not feel that way.

Eliza had learned more about weather in the past twenty-four hours than she had in the previous thirty-six years. Pressure, temperature. Wind shear, projection models. Seasonal shifts in the flow of the ocean. She felt dumb for admitting this, but she didn't even know that the ocean flowed at all. Didn't it just kind of ... sit there? Not quite, as it turned out. It flowed, and in the case of Hurricane Brenda, it flowed in such a way as to bring a vicious storm right to Nantucket's doorstep.

Oliver was doing his best to calm her down. He brought her a cup of hot tea with honey when he found her hunched over the computer first thing Wednesday morning with about forty internet browser tabs open. She'd looked up at him, hair and eyes wild, and said, "Did you know that a hurricane can dump more than 2.4 trillion gallons of rain in a day?"

"Liza," he'd replied, "take a deep breath. Everything is going to be fine."

"The statistical models don't agree with you." She waved a hand dismissively and turned back to the screen to refresh again and again until the hourly update from the National Weather Service popped up.

The rest of the day was similarly unproductive. Every time she closed her eyes, she saw driving rains, lashing winds, trees being uprooted. She saw her wedding dress being torn to shreds and ripped out to sea by hurricane-force gales.

This was a nightmare in the making.

But by the time sunset came around, she was forced to take a break from hurricane hunting and hop into the shower. Oliver's adoptive parents, Neal and Marcy, were due to arrive in town shortly for the wedding festivities. She and Oliver were going to go meet them for dinner to welcome them in.

Eliza's mind was still on the storm as she blow-dried and straightened her hair, then pulled on a slim-fitting gray dress and black ballet flats. That was the main reason she felt so wound up. There was also the usual pressure of interacting with the parents of your significant other, no matter how many times they'd gotten together before. Even at thirty-six years old, it still held a little bit of trepidation for her.

Mom arrived around 7:30 to babysit Winter while she and Oliver were out to eat. "Thanks, Mae," Oliver said, kissing Mae on the cheek after they'd gotten her all settled in. "We shouldn't be much later than 9:30 or 10."

Eliza was tapping her foot nervously by the door. "What's up with you, hon?" Mom asked, casting a concerned glance in her direction.

Oliver rolled his eyes. "Don't even start," he warned her. "That's a can of worms you do *not* want to open, trust me."

"I'm right here, you know," Eliza snapped. "With functioning ears and everything."

Mom's eyes widened. "Well, you all have a lovely dinner!" she said with a bright smile that said *Never mind, I don't want to know.* She ushered them to the door. "And Oliver, darling, tell your parents that I am so excited to see them again."

"Will do. Don't be afraid to give us a call if Winter starts throwing a fit. She's had a couple doozies lately."

"We'll be all smiles over here, I assure you. Bye-bye!"

The door shut firmly behind them.

Oliver chuckled. "Smart lady," he muttered.

"What?"

"Nothing. Not a thing at all. Let's go eat!" He rubbed his hands together as they walked towards the car and headed off to dinner.

The drive downtown was short. Oliver found a primo parking spot, right out front of the restaurant, and pulled in. He killed the ignition, but just before he got out, Eliza grabbed his forearm.

"Wait a second." She looked at him. She was stunned to realize that she had tears brimming in the corners of her eyes. Jeez, she had been so emotional lately! Obviously, no bride wants their wedding day ruined by a hurricane. But this felt like an overreaction, even to her. There was still plenty of time for the storm to change course and miss Nantucket entirely. It was looking less and less likely with every passing hour, but it wasn't yet out of the question.

Oliver looked back at her, eyes flashing in the headlights of passing cars. He said nothing, just waited patiently for Eliza to find the words.

"Everything is going to be okay, right?" She wasn't an idiot—she knew very well that Oliver hadn't the faintest idea about what the hurricane was going to do, if their wedding would be messed up, any of that. But right here, right now, she very badly needed some reassurance.

He laid his hand gently over the top of hers. He didn't blink as he said, "Eliza, baby, I promise you this: everything is going to be absolutely perfect."

She nodded and sniffled, then dabbed at the tears threatening to spill over the corners of her eyes. "You mean it?"

"I mean it," he said. "Trust me."

"Okay." He meant it, she could tell. He wasn't just lying to make her feel better. He genuinely, actually, one-hundred-percent meant what he said.

That was good. That made one of them who still believed things were going to work out. Better than none, she supposed.

Now was the time to pull herself together, though. Neal and Marcy were waiting.

She'd met them last year around Christmas, when she and Oliver took Winter down to Connecticut for a long weekend, and they'd chitchatted via FaceTime sporadically over the last year. But she still felt a little nervous around them. There was no real reason to feel that way. Both of them were perfectly nice, perfectly friendly, pretty much exactly what she'd expected from suburban Connecticuters who both worked at a dentist's office. She took a deep breath and blinked the tears away.

"Ready?" Oliver asked, smiling.

"Ready," she confirmed. They got out of the car. Eliza twined her fingers through Oliver's and held him close as they walked up to the restaurant.

Neal and Marcy were seated in the waiting area when they stepped inside. "There's our rock star!" Neal said. He turned to Eliza. "And his muse!" The four of them all swapped hugs around and said the usual things about how good each of them looked.

Neal was balding on top and graying on the sides, with enough of a middle-aged-man potbelly to test the limits of the belt looped through his dark blue slacks. He had glasses that barely hung onto the edge of his nose and a smile that was infectiously warm. He'd recently started growing out his beard—"it's what the kids are doing these days" was his reasoning, apparently. Marcy always made fun of him, but she'd admitted privately to Eliza that she was starting to like it a little bit.

Marcy was wearing a black three-quarter-sleeve blazer over jeans and some sparkly high heels. She was a snappy dresser, though Eliza always thought that she wore an awful lot of jewelry. Oliver had mentioned more than once that going through airport security with her was headache-inducing. Tonight, Eliza counted five and six bracelets on each wrist, respectively, a blinding gold necklace, and two earrings per ear.

"Patterson, party of four?" the hostess called over from the check-in desk with a smile and a wave. "Your table is ready, if you'll follow me right this way."

They filed over to their table and settled in.

"So!" Neal said, rubbing his hands together just like Oliver had when they were leaving the house. "Tell me what's good here."

"Dad, you've been here before," Oliver groaned.

"Have I?"

"Yes, honey!" Marcy said. "Don't you remember? Two Thanksgivings ago! That was pre-Eliza, though. I think Amanda was still in the picture back then."

"Mom!" Oliver cut in sharply.

Eliza blushed and laughed. "It's okay."

"No, it's not okay," Oliver corrected. "Anyway, moving on. I'd get the lobster or the mussels, Dad."

"I did like Amanda ..." Neal muttered under his breath absentmindedly.

Marcy whacked him in the arm. "He just asked us not to talk about her! Clean out your ears, Neal."

Oliver buried his face in his hands. Eliza's blush deepened.

Things were off to a great start.

Fortunately, they stabilized after that. They got a lot of conversational mileage out of picking over every single item on the menu, and then the usual chatter about Winter: what new tricks she was learning, what things she could do, as if she was a dog. That phrasing always slightly bothered Eliza—"what can she do now?"—but she didn't intend on making a fuss.

Appetizers, wine, and main courses came and went. Eliza was hungry and the food was good, though she still didn't feel like drinking too much. When they were all almost done eating, Oliver started poking his dad about a story he loved bringing up—the time when Neal had tried to clean the chimney at their house in Connecticut by himself, without consulting anyone on proper chimney-cleaning protocol.

"And then he came down with his face covered—I mean, absolutely freaking *covered*—in soot. I have never laughed harder," Oliver finished. Marcy, too, was laughing, and Neal was chuckling at his own expense, though Eliza saw that he maybe wasn't as fond of this story as his adoptive son was.

Marcy had been a little harsh on Neal throughout the meal, in Eliza's opinion. Not anything malicious, just the normal picking and poking of a couple who had been together for a very long time. But Eliza thought that Neal was getting a little flustered and irritated with her chirping at him so incessantly. Marcy leaned back in her chair at the conclusion of Oliver's retelling of the chimney story and said, "I swear, Neal, you used to be the laziest man on this planet. And then somehow you got lazier!" Eliza saw a switch flip in Neal's head.

His face got red and splotchy as he blurted out, "At least I'm not as lazy as his father!" His finger jabbed towards Oliver. "That son of a gun *still* won't get a job!"

Everyone froze.

Silence. It felt like the whole restaurant was holding its breath. Eliza wasn't sure how much time passed. Ten seconds? Ten minutes? Ten hours?

Neal's finger was still hovering over the tabletop in Oliver's direction when Marcy's furious, hissed, "NEAL!" broke the spell of silence.

Eliza's gaze flew to Oliver. He was frozen stiff, all the color gone from his face. She didn't move a muscle. She just watched him process what Neal had said and the implication of his phrasing.

Finally, Oliver said what everyone was thinking: "My father is alive?"

Silence.

Neal was still red, but no longer with anger. It was the face of a man who knew he had just said something very, very wrong. Marcy's bracelets were jangling under the table—Eliza could hear them. The jangling of gold bracelets and the tap-tap-tap of her high heels on the hardwood floor and, in the background, the clatter and tinkle of plates being set down and drinks being poured at the table behind them.

But at their table, no one said a word.

Not until Oliver repeated what he'd said. "My father is alive?"

Neal's lips were quivering. "Well ..."

Oliver shook his head. "You told me he was dead. You said he and my mom were both dead."

"Oliver, honey ..." Marcy said.

He immediately held up a hand to cut her off. "No. I want to hear him answer my question. You told me my father was dead. My whole life, you said he was dead. Is he dead or not?"

"He's alive," Neal whispered. His gaze was aimed straight down in his lap. His face was still red and sweat had begun to roll down his temple. Eliza was starting to worry that the collar of his shirt was too tight. He looked like he was suffering immensely.

"He's alive," Oliver echoed numbly. He nodded like he was taking this in, adding a new puzzle piece to his worldview. "My father is alive. Okay. Where is he?"

"Darling, we don't know—"

"Liar." Oliver's harsh tone was a brutal knife swipe cutting through Marcy's pleas. She reeled back like he'd hurt her physically.

Silence again.

Eliza didn't know what to do or say. She didn't know if *anyone* knew what to do or so. They were all watching Oliver and waiting.

"Where is he?" he asked again. He was using a quiet, venomous voice Eliza had never heard from him before. It frightened her to the core. His thigh was close enough to hers that she could sense his leg bouncing violently.

"He's in Philadelphia," Neal answered. He had yet to look up.

"I want an address."

Marcy began, "We don't have—"

"Liar."

Eliza saw Neal flinch this time when Oliver said that word. As if he had been struck across the face.

Neal mumbled an address. It was obvious that he'd memorized it a long time ago. This was a secret that had been buried for a very long time.

Oliver stood up suddenly. His chair screeched. Reaching into his pocket, he withdrew two hundred-dollar bills and threw them down on the table. "Thanks for dinner," he said in that same deadly quiet voice. "I'm going to go find my father now."

He turned and left.

Eliza looked at Neal and Marcy. Both of them were looking into their laps now. She thought she saw tears mingling with the sweat on Neal's face, but she wasn't sure. She hesitated for just one more second before getting up and following Oliver out the door.

"Oliver!" she called after him into the night. She could see his figure crossing the street in the darkness. He didn't turn around. Cursing under her breath, she checked for oncoming traffic, then ran across the street.

She caught up with him as he reached for the car door handle. "Oliver, baby, look at me." He didn't do it. Just kept staring down at her hand seizing his forearm. She said it again. "Oliver, please look at me."

This time, he looked up at her. He was crying.

"I have to go find him," he told her in a voice that was strong despite the tears. The venom that had laced his words just moments before was gone. In its place was a trembling fear she'd never heard from him before, either. In all the time they'd been together, he'd never been this vulnerable.

A billion thoughts careened through her head at once. They had a wedding in four days, and yet her soon-to-be-husband was about to get in the car and drive to Philadelphia to chase down the father he thought was long dead. She wanted to be mad that he was abandoning her. But she knew that wouldn't be right. She had his love already. The wedding wasn't as important as that, surely?

No, it wasn't. This thing right here mattered. It mattered as much as anything Oliver had ever done. She could see the thousand-yard stare on his face that told her that explicitly. He needed to go. So she swallowed her sadness, her anger, her bewilderment—how could all this be happening *now* of all times?—and she nodded. She had tears of her own in her eyes.

"Okay," she whispered. "I love you, okay, Oliver?"

He nodded back. "I love you too, Eliza. I'll be home soon."

She stepped back and let him go. She would call a taxi to get home.

Oliver needed to go.

15

HOLLY

Holly stumbled out of Cecilia's house like she was drunk. Her head was still reeling with the whiplash suddenness of everything that had just happened. She heard the door click behind her, but she didn't look back.

She drove home in a daze. When she pulled into her driveway, she blinked and realized that she didn't remember a single moment of the journey from the Paynes' house back to hers. Like someone had snipped the film out of her memory reel. It was unnerving.

The pain on Cecilia's face was etched into Holly's mind's eye. There was loss in her eyes, loss for something she'd never had and never would have. It shook Holly to her core.

She forced herself to get out of the car. The silence in there was too stifling. Outside, the night was buzzing with the warm creak of cicadas and the distant wash of the ocean. It was clear, cool, beautiful.

"Take a step," she said to herself. It was like she had to manually pick up each leg and place it in front. Things weren't working, weren't connecting. Somehow, she made it up the driveway and to the front door. She paused there for a moment and drew in a long, shuddering breath.

The door opened before she could open it herself. Pete was on the other side, grinning. He waggled his cell phone at her proudly. "Saw you on the cameras ..." he began. But his grin fell to a frown when he saw how shell-shocked his wife looked. "Honey, are you okay?"

She didn't say anything for one long second. Then, feeling a surge of something new and warm rush into her, she stepped forward and squeezed her husband in the tightest hug she could muster.

She felt like she could stay in his arms forever. With her ear pressed against his chest, she heard his heartbeat. *Ba-boom. Ba-boom.* Steady, dependable. He was warm and he smelled like Pete. His two-day beard scratched the top of her head, but she couldn't care less. *Grow it a foot long if you want,* she thought of telling him. *Just don't go anywhere, okay? Stay with me here. Don't let go of this hug.* She decided not to say that out loud. She just held him for a long time.

He finally let go of her and stepped back. "Everything all right?"

She smiled up at him. "I just missed you. That's all."

He frowned—she knew he didn't believe her—but he didn't press the subject. She appreciated that more than he would ever know. She wasn't sure how to put her feelings into words just yet.

She turned to face the living room. Grady was playing video games on the couch. Alice was reading a book. She went over and pressed a soft kiss onto her head, then his. She lingered for as long as she could get away with without offending either one. They were almost past the age where they craved Mommy's love, so she was glad that they let her do this now. She needed it badly. She needed to smell her kids and her husband, to feel their body heat, to see them blink and breathe and laugh. It mattered so, so much all of a sudden. She was blessed. She didn't need the dream house or anything else at all, so long as she had these things.

"Do you guys want to go get ice cream?" she asked suddenly, jangling her keys. "Mom's treat." Pete was an automatic yes, she knew.

Grady and Alice both looked up at her. "On a school night?" Alice squealed.

"Our little secret," she replied.

Both of them looked at each other, then back at her with huge smiles on their faces. They dropped what they were doing and sprinted to put their shoes on at the door. Holly rested her head on Pete's shoulder while she watched them squabble to get ready. She could already tell that this stupid, silly moment would be one that she remembered forever.

At the ice-cream place, Holly got pistachio with sprinkles. Pete got chocolate with chocolate syrup. Alice and Grady both got the most violently rainbow-colored flavor they could find. Holly let them get large sizes, too, so they were both over the moon.

On the way back home, she cranked the song playing on the one CD she kept in her car—"Bohemian Rhapsody" by Queen. She'd been playing it since the kids were born, for a moment just like this—when everybody sang together. Grady and Pete teamed up for the low parts while Alice and Holly did the falsettos. They all sang the hook at the end at the top of their lungs, as a Nantucket summer breeze blew in through the open windows and the sweetness of ice cream hummed on their tongues.

A sudden memory hit Holly like a runaway train. She was in the car on a night like this. It was before the kids were born, so it was just her and Pete. He was about a year out from college and working a dead-end corporate job he hated. She was a secretary in the vault of a bank. They were young and in love and poor as all get-out. She remembered this moment specifically because Pete had won a raffle at his office for a free dinner at some steakhouse in town. On the way back, they were driving and singing along to the radio, buzzing with wine and free food and each other. They'd pulled into the parking garage of the crummy apartment they were staying at while they searched for somewhere better that wasn't outrageously expensive. It was pitch dark—the lights never worked in here. When Pete killed the engine, she grabbed his wrist and looked at him, though she couldn't see much.

"I have to tell you something," she said that night. Her eyes were glistening.

"Lemme guess," he said. "You're joining the circus."

She giggled. "Strike one."

"Your long-lost great-great aunt just left us a billion-dollar inheritance."

"Ooh, good guess. Strike two, though."

"You're pregnant."

She bit her lip, then smiled. "Bingo."

He did a double take. His jaw fell. "No way."

"Hit it out of the park, babe."

"Stop."

"The crowd's going crazy."

"No."

She hesitated. Then a car rounded the corner and lit him up with its headlights and she saw that he had a smile stretching from ear to ear.

"You're happy, right?" she asked.

He put a hand on the side of her face and pulled his forehead up to touch hers. She felt his breath on her lips, warm and fragrant with the tang of red wine.

"I've never been happier, Hollz."

That was how she felt now. Like she'd never been happier.

They made a blanket fort when they got home. Pete and Alice read books. Holly and Grady played video games together until all of them were drooping. One by one, the kids and then Pete fell asleep. Holly was the last one awake. Eyes lidded with the weight of the sugar crash, she looked around and saw the rising and falling chests of her family as they slumbered.

She smiled to herself. Then she fell asleep, too.

16

BRENT

Just after dawn on Thursday morning.
Three days until Eliza's wedding.

∽

"I'm dying. For real. This is the end. Bury me here."

"Quit your whining, Marsh. If you were dying, you wouldn't be able to talk so dang much."

Marshall was hunched over, hands on his knees, taking in huge, gasping breaths like he'd just run a marathon. Brent stood by with his arms crossed over his chest, watching his melodramatic friend ham it up for an audience of—well, it was just Brent and Henrietta here on the beach with him. It was just a few minutes after dawn on Thursday morning. They had been out on the sand and loosening up before the sun finally peeked over the horizon.

Marshall straightened up and took in one more slow, aching inhale, as if it was the last one he'd ever get to take. "When did you become the Flash?" he asked.

Brent chuckled. Henrietta pawed the sand impatiently. "We ran a mile in twelve minutes. I wouldn't exactly call that 'top speed,' amigo."

His best friend fixed him with the most utterly serious stare he could muster. "I am extremely confident that what we just did was a world record."

Brent rolled his eyes and checked his watch again. "C'mon, we got three more miles at least until I let you call it quits."

Marshall's jaw dropped. "Three more of those? You are out of your mind, Triple B. Wait, where are you going? Don't start running again!"

But Brent and Henrietta were already a few yards away down the beach, settling back into a gentle jog and laughing under their breath as Marshall scrambled to catch up.

It had become a new morning routine. Or rather, it was going to be, as soon as Marshall quit being such a whiny little crybaby about the whole thing. Brent would've thought, after years of hauling in fish, scrubbing hulls, and doing all the other little manual tasks that running a charter fishing business required, that Marshall would be more physically fit. He had been wrong. Marshall was sucking wind within seconds of setting off on this morning's run, which he intended to be the first of many. But he was still jabbering as per usual, so Brent didn't take him too seriously just yet.

They made their way another two and a half miles before Marshall stopped talking altogether and just started staring at the horizon as they plodded ahead, like a shell-shocked soldier coming home from the battlefield. That was when Brent knew that he was nearing the end of his rope.

But it was such a beautiful morning that he thought it was a shame to give up so early. There'd been a lot of talk around town about this Hurricane Brenda that seemed to be bearing down on

Nantucket. Brent figured, if they were going to get jacked up by a vicious storm like that, he might as well enjoy the pretty weather while it lasted.

Marshall agreed—right up until the point when he didn't. At long last, Brent slowed to a walk and then stopped. Marshall promptly collapsed on the ground like he'd been shot by a sniper. Brent laughed and stood over him.

"How we doin', Marsh?"

"Tell my mother I love her."

"You gonna be able to walk home?"

Marshall cracked open one eye and glared at him. "Just make sure the Med-Evac helicopter has room to land, okay?"

Henrietta licked the salty sweat off his face. Marshall didn't have the energy to push her away.

"He's not getting up anytime soon, is he?" Brent asked her. She whined, which he interpreted as agreement. Sighing, he took a seat on the sand next to his buddy and looked out across the water. "It's a beautiful place we live in, ain't it, Marsh?"

"Mmf."

"We're lucky to be here."

"Urgh."

"Sun is shining, breeze is blowing, summer is in full effect."

"Blargh."

He glanced over. "You're not gonna puke, are you?"

"No comment."

"Well, at least we're speaking in full sentences again. C'mere, girl," he said to Henrietta. She came over and laid her head in his lap for him to pet. "I'm thankful for you, too," he said, leaning down to kiss her between the ears. "You came into my life at the right time."

They sat in silence and enjoyed the morning for a while. Gradually, Marshall revived and struggled back upright. By now, the sun was well above the horizon and it was time to get the day started. The two men clasped hands and pulled each other to their feet.

Marshall dusted himself off and squinted around. "Can't wait until we do this again next year."

"I think you mean tomorrow, friendo."

He blanched. "I'll consider myself lucky if I can even *walk* tomorrow," he protested.

"You're a lucky guy. And either way, you're getting three miles done with me. Bright and early."

"You are the bane of my existence, Triple B."

"I love you too, Marsh."

Together, they trudged up the beach towards the pathway that wound between the dunes. Henrietta ran ahead, in an unusually good mood compared to how unfriendly she'd been lately. She still had a lot of energy, since they hadn't done the five or six miles that Brent normally ran. Marshall wasn't quite ready for that.

"What's on the agenda today?" Brent asked.

"Well," Marshall began, scratching his chin, "after this little warm-up we did, I was thinking we'd tackle five thousand push-ups, ten thousand squats, a million chin-ups, then some—"

"Wait." Brent froze. "Did you hear that?"

"Over the sound of my own physical excellence? I don't think so."

Suddenly, Brent realized the source of the yelping noise he'd just heard. He looked around. Henrietta must have run past the bend up ahead. He took off sprinting.

When he rounded the corner, he saw her lying on her side and whining.

He also saw the quick flash of a snake slithering back into the underbrush.

"Henrietta!" He bounded over and fell to his knees next to her. The sounds coming out of her throat were garbled and pained. His eyes scanned over her and saw two pinpricks of blood on her belly.

Marshall came lumbering around the bend moments later.

Brent looked up and made eye contact. "She got bit by a snake," he said. "We need to her to the vet. Now!"

The ride to the veterinarian's office was rushed and horrible. Brent sat in the back seat with Henrietta on his lap. She'd stopped making noise altogether. Her chest was still rising and falling, so he knew she could still breathe, but he swore he could sense the poison spreading throughout her body. If he could find that snake, he'd chop it into a billion pieces and scatter them in every corner of the planet.

But first, he needed to make sure that his favorite companion would survive.

"Drive faster, Marsh!" he barked.

"I'm going as fast as I can, B. We're almost there. Is it a left or a right here?"

"Left! Left! Go left!"

Marshall wrenched the wheel around and then they squealed into the parking lot. Brent was out of the car before it came to a full stop, bearing Henrietta in his arms. He kicked the door in lieu of knocking, over and over until someone finally answered.

"Hi, yes, we heard you—" the vet began, but Brent was already pushing his way through.

"Snakebite," he said through the haze of his panic. "You gotta hurry!"

Fear had a firm handhold on his guts and was squeezing the life out of him. He laid Henrietta down on the cold metal examination table where the vet, Dr. Lena Dawson, directed him. She had snapped into business mode immediately when she saw the look on Brent's face.

"Her, here. You, there." She pointed towards a chair through the doorway into the other room.

"No," he said immediately. "I'm staying with her."

Dr. Dawson shook her head. "I can't do my job if you're in here hovering. Go sit."

Marshall had come in behind him. "C'mon, B," he said softly. "Just come sit."

Brent let Marshall lead him away. The door closed behind him. The two of them sat down in the rigid waiting room chairs. Brent stared between his feet, face white. Marshall patted him on the back once or twice, then they fell silent.

Half an hour passed in the blink of an eye. Brent hadn't moved. Had hardly breathed, as a matter of fact. How much loss was he going to have to take in his life? Every time he thought he was through the worst of it, he got beaten back down. Henrietta was innocent. She was a good dog, the best dog. She deserved better than this. He couldn't bear the thought of losing her. He prayed that Dr. Dawson knew what she was doing.

Finally, the door swung back open. Dr. Dawson reemerged, stripping off rubber gloves.

Brent looked up, eyes full of equal parts fear and hope. "Please tell me she's okay," he said immediately.

Dr. Dawson smiled. "She's going to be fine," she said. "I gave her a mild sedative, so she's sleeping a little bit for right now. Didn't want her to be distressed with all the chaos going on."

Brent buried his face in his hands. He wanted to cry. But this was neither the time nor the place. He took a deep breath, stored away his relief for later, and looked up once again.

"Thank you," he whispered.

"It's a good thing you got her here so quickly."

"That'd be my doing, ma'am," Marshall said. He raised his hand like a kid in class. "Best driver north of the Mason-Dixon Line, or so I've been told."

Brent looked over at his friend in disbelief. If he didn't know any better, he'd say Marshall was flirting with the vet.

He glanced back over to Dr. Dawson and saw, to his even greater surprise, that she was laughing. "Is that a fact?" she said. "Well, the dog is certainly lucky to have the two of you, then."

Brent thought about being mad for a second. But then he thought better of it. Henrietta was going to be just fine—the doc had just said so. The worst had passed.

So instead, he took stock of the situation. Dr. Dawson was tall, slender, with dark hair pulled back in a no-nonsense ponytail. Between that, the glasses, and the white lab coat she was wearing, she had a whole "competent professional" vibe that he figured Marshall found attractive.

For his part, Marshall was sweating like a pig after their morning run, but hey, the guy did have a certain kind of motormouth charm, right? And Brent knew how lonely his best friend felt sometimes. For all that people like Marshall—friendly and charismatic—seemed to be casual buddies with everybody, they often didn't have many folks they could truly talk to and connect with on a deeper level. Maybe this wasn't such a bad thing at all.

That being said, he wasn't going to sit around while they made goo-goo eyes at each other. "Can I go see her?" he asked.

"Go right ahead," Dr. Dawson replied. "I'll wait out here for you."

Brent swept in, leaving the doc and Marshall together outside.

Like she'd said, Henrietta was asleep on the exam table. She was breathing slowly and easily, much better than the rapid-fire shallow breaths she'd been taking in the car ride on the way here. He saw that the area of the snakebite had been shaved and smeared with a white ointment that was peeking out around the edges of the bandage. He let out a sigh of relief. It was one thing to hear that she was going to be okay, and another thing to see it.

Bending over, he buried his face in her neck and took a deep breath. She smelled like *her*: like sandy beach and dog and sunshine. He was glad she wasn't going anywhere.

He hung out in there for a little while, petting her softly and watching her sleep. His fear gradually receded back to where it had come from. He heard the muffled voices of Marshall and the vet outside. Eventually, he opened the door and stuck his head back out.

"Can I take her home?" he asked.

Dr. Dawson was next to Marshall in the seat that Brent had vacated. She looked up at him and nodded with a smile. "I'll need to see her again tomorrow for some follow-up exams. But she should be good for the evening. Just keep a close eye on her, all right?"

Brent gave her a thumbs-up. Then he picked Henrietta up gingerly and took her out to the car. "Let's go home, girl," he whispered in her ear. He could almost swear she smiled at that.

Brent didn't leave Henrietta's side for the rest of the day. He took her to Rose's instead of his apartment, so he could bring her outside if she felt like running around. But she kept sleeping for a long time. When she woke up around sunset, he put some food and water out for her. She didn't eat much, but he made sure she drank enough to stay hydrated. Then she went back to sleep.

Rose came home shortly after. He explained everything that had happened.

"Oh, I'm so sorry, babe!" she exclaimed. She'd pulled him into a tight hug. "I'm glad she's going to be okay."

"Me too," he murmured. "But I think I'm gonna sleep down here tonight, just so I can be close to her."

Rose nodded. "Yeah, of course."

She cooked dinner for her and Susanna. She offered Brent some food, too, but he wasn't very hungry, so he passed.

Day turned to night and Henrietta kept sleeping. Every time her belly paused for even a second at the end of an inhale or an exhale, Brent held his own breath until she resumed.

Oddly enough, it made him think of the conversation that he and Rose had after he stopped by her classroom on Monday. *You were great with the kids,* she'd said.

He remembered something Eliza had said to him, too, about watching Winter sleep just after she was born. *I can't breathe until she does,* she'd said. *Every breath is terrifying because of that.*

That was being a parent, it seemed. Watching every twitch, every breath, every single moment and wondering if this was the first or the best or the worst or the last. Constant, rending anxiety clawing away at your insides. Responsibility weighing on your shoulders like gravity had doubled. That was a lot to handle.

But as he looked at Henrietta where she lay, he felt suddenly okay with that burden. Because there was joy here, too, in the good moments. In seeing her pant and bark and run alongside him on the beach in the morning. Seeing her rub her cold nose up against Susanna's face and making the little girl giggle.

Those things made the fear worth it.

You were great with the kids.

Maybe he could be.

17

MAE

Going to the beach with Dominic and Saoirse was the last thing that Mae wanted to do. And yet, here she was, headed for a sunset stroll with her boyfriend on one side and his ex-wife on the other.

How on earth had she ended up in this situation? Just a few short days ago, this had all the makings of a beautiful and memorable week. Now, not so much. Hurricanes and ex-wives had come storming ashore. Mae wasn't sure which one she was less excited about.

"You are from here, yes?" Saoirse asked suddenly, turning to Mae. It had taken every ounce of Mae's willpower to stay walking alongside her. She was stuck in the middle of this hideously awkward trio and hating every second of it.

"Yes," Mae answered. "Well, actually, not quite. I'm from Tennessee originally."

"So you are not from here, then."

"Uh, I guess not. It sure feels like I am, though!" Mae tried to grit out a smile as best she could. This woman was really testing her patience.

But, in between bouts of irritation, she almost wanted to laugh at herself. She had a flashback to a conversation between herself and Sara when her daughter was in high school. Sara had gotten into a few spats with another girl in her class. It was over something silly that Mae couldn't quite recall. A parking space in the school lot, perhaps, or maybe it was about which color dress one or the other of the girls was going to wear to prom. Something petty, but, with typical Sara gung-ho, she had promptly decided to hate everything about this girl, this new nemesis. She ranted and raved to her mother about the way the girl wore her hair, her laugh, the shoddy state of her backpack, her choice of shoes.

Mae remembered listening to Sara wear herself out with complaining, before gently pointing out that Sara wore her hair similarly, laughed just as loud when the mood struck, refused to zip her backpack in much the same way, and had just a week ago requested a pair of those exact same shoes. Sara didn't like that answer, of course. It had devolved into another fight between them. But the whole thing had always struck Mae as kind of funny. No detail or quirk of personality is too small to be despised in those we dislike.

That was how she felt about Saoirse in this moment. The way the woman alternated between blunt and cryptic drove Mae up the wall. Gold earrings with a silver necklace? Tacky. *Stop touching my boyfriend's arm!* she screamed inside her head. On and on like that, an ugly merry-go-round of petty little grievances.

And now, here she was, putting Mae through the wringer of question after question like she was being deposed. Add that to the list as well.

"How do you mean?" Saoirse asked.

Mae blinked. "I'm sorry?"

"You said, 'It feels like I am, though.' What does that mean?"

Mae glanced over at Dominic, who had remained steadfastly silent pretty much since the moment of Saoirse's arrival. She wondered if he knew that he was hanging Mae out to dry. To be fair, he looked like he was suffering, too. Why, though? Any former lover can bring up unseen tensions, of course, especially when they show up with little advance notice, as Saoirse had done. But if Mae had to say, she would think that the look on Dominic's face was something different.

"I suppose I just mean that I love Nantucket. That's all," Mae answered simply.

What was this woman trying to drag out of her? A confession that she wasn't actually a native of the island? What good would that do—and more to the point, who cared?

"I see."

There we go again, Mae thought. *From blunt to cryptic at the drop of a hat. What does she want from me? From us? From this visit?* All she had was questions, and Saoirse did not seem interested in supplying answers.

They reached the beach entrance and made their way through the dunes. Breaking out onto the expanse of the beach, Mae inhaled the scent of the salty breeze and sighed. Coming out here always felt like aloe on a sunburn. It was true that she wasn't from Nantucket. But she felt deep in her bones that she belonged here. She spoke the same language that this place did, like she was part and parcel of the land itself. The acrid tang of low tide mixed with the raspy dryness of the sand all just felt *right* to her. She thought of her parents' old farm, landlocked in the heart of Tennessee, and sighed again. That was home, too, but in a very different way. Not like this.

"'Though we travel the world over to find the beautiful, we must carry it with us, or we find it not.'"

Mae's head whirled to her right, where Dominic stood facing the water, his hands clasped behind his back.

"What did you just say?" she asked him.

"It is a quote from Emerson," he murmured.

"What does it mean?"

He didn't say anything.

Questions, questions, questions. No one seemed interested in answering any of them.

And Mae had had about enough of it.

"It is a beautiful evening," she said firmly, "but I think I ought to be getting home now to start dinner."

She looked at Dominic. He didn't say anything or return her gaze.

Lord, she could give him a good talking-to right now! It would have to wait for later, though. Mae was a firm believer that couples ought to handle their issues behind closed doors. No matter how mad she was at Dominic for springing this whole situation upon her and then abandoning her to deal with Saoirse herself, she wasn't going to wring him out in front of their guest.

She turned to look at Saoirse and gave her a firm nod as well. Saoirse wasn't looking back, though. She was staring out over the water with an inscrutable look in her eyes.

The two of them deserve each other! Mae thought to herself angrily. It felt like there were secrets swirling around in the air, being conveyed in a frequency that she didn't know how to decipher. There were many things to which she could attribute that feeling of being left out. Both of them were Irish; both of them were once married to each other. But the rationale she kept coming back to, over and over, was that they had a permanent bond between them that Mae was encroaching upon. She felt like she had touched it and instinctively recoiled, same as if she'd reached her hand out and laid a finger upon an electric fence. Whatever was happening, she wasn't privy to it.

Fine. So be it. She'd just get going then, and leave these two ex-lovers to be cryptically silent in each other's company. She was fed up with wasting her time here.

She turned to leave. But before she took even a single step towards home, Saoirse grabbed her forearm. "Mae," she said. "Walk with me."

"Ask Dominic," Mae snapped. As before, she cringed inside at how rude she was being. But the time for manners had come and gone. If they were going to be cold to her, well, she didn't exactly feel like being Mrs. Warm-and-Hospitable to them.

"I'd like *you* to walk with me," Saoirse said, putting extra emphasis on the word *you.*

Mae didn't know what to make of that. There was a forcefulness about this woman when she chose to extend it. Mae found that unsettling, if only because she had none of that in her. She wasn't a pushover, by any means, but Saoirse seemed to have this river of— what? Rage? Sorrow? Bitterness? Mae didn't know, but there was *something* in Saoirse that was both alluring and scary.

Mae let out a long, slow exhale. "All right," she said, feeling defeated. What else was there to do?

Saoirse nodded, then turned on her heel and started down the beach without waiting to see if Mae was joining her.

She took a few quick steps to catch up, then glanced back over her shoulder at Dominic. He was still standing exactly as he had been, unmoving like a statue, hands behind his back, with that look in his eyes like he was staring far beyond the waves.

18

SARA

Thursday night.

～

They were short one chef on the prep line tonight since Ricky was sick, so Sara was filling in. It was a nice change of pace to get her hands dirty for once. She'd started her career doing stuff like this: peeling potatoes, deboning fish, plating appetizers. With all the thoughts that had been swirling through her mind in the last days and weeks, she was appreciative of the chance to just do the work and not worry about all that. These were the kind of simple, binary tasks that she loved. You just peeled the potato. There was no need to agonize over it. Do the dang thing, then the next, then the next. It made her think of a sort-of-joke about an old Buddhist monk that her dad used to tell all the time. It went something like:

There was an old Buddhist monk meditating on top of a mountain. One day, a young man made his way up there to seek the monk's wisdom.

"Master," he asked, "what did you do before you became enlightened?"

"Before enlightenment, the laundry," answered the old monk.

"And what did you do after you became enlightened?"

The old monk smiled. "After enlightenment, the laundry."

The gist of the story—at least, in the way her dad had explained it—was that there was as much meaning in a task as you brought to it. The task remained the task. Chop the wood, carry the water, do the laundry, peel the potato. That always made Sara feel good about chores like this, for some reason. It was like running a marathon and telling yourself, "One step at a time."

While she peeled yet another, a subtle smile on her face, Cassandra came up to tell her that her cell phone had been ringing off the hook in her office. "It won't quit," she said. "Must be important."

"Thanks, Cass," Sara said. "Be right there." She washed her hands real quick and then went into her office to see what the fuss was about.

Her cell phone had actually vibrated its way off her desk and down to the floor. Sighing, she reached down and scooped it up. She saw that she had about fifteen missed calls from a New York number, and an email at the top of her inbox marked "URGENT." She frowned and hit the email first.

As she read what it said, her eyes bulged.

She dialed the number back immediately.

"Benny?" she said when the man at the other end of the line answered.

"Sara, thank God, I've been trying to reach you." Benny was a server at Lonesome Dove, the New York City restaurant owned by Gavin Crawford that Sara had once worked at. They had kept in touch on and off over the last couple years.

"Sorry, we're short a prep cook tonight. Are you serious with what you sent me?"

"Dead serious," he confirmed. "I need your help. I don't know what to do with this stuff."

Sara sank into the chair behind her desk and closed her eyes. They were going to have to proceed very, very carefully.

Because the email that Benny sent her contained everything she needed in order to make Gavin Crawford pay for what he'd done to her.

When the call was over, Sara sat in the stillness of her office for a minute and thought. Then she checked the clock. Dinner service was almost upon them. She needed to get back to her station.

But the peace and serenity she'd had before was gone. She racked her brain over what to do with the information in Benny's email.

It was a complex batch of documents, but the basic takeaway was this: Gavin was hiding major losses at his restaurant group with illegal accounting. Benny, who'd recently been promoted to a kind of business manager/front-of-house hybrid role, had discovered a second set of books while doing some cleanup on one of the restaurant's old computers. These, as compared to the official accounting records that Gavin shared with his co-owners and investors, showed massive expenditures on "entertainment" that Benny suspected were going straight into Gavin's pockets. Cars, apartments, flights, meals and drinks out on the town ... the list went on and on. It was extensive and damaging. And, in the notoriously tight-knit world of fine dining, if it became public, it would absolutely trash Gavin's reputation. No one would ever want to work with him again. The food world tolerated a lot of character defects in its citizens, but one thing it did not tolerate was thieving.

All of that meant one thing: Sara could ruin him.

That was a lot of power in her hands. Her first thought was to get a newspaper on the phone right now. Gavin's restaurants were extremely well-known throughout the northeast United States. Anyone with a foot in the industry would want to know about this. The right reporter could really blow it all out of the water. Sara salivated at the thought of seeing Gavin's name splashed over newspapers across the country. *Decorated Restauranteur Embezzling from Partners* had a delicious ring to it. Or maybe something punnier, more New York Post-style: *Restaurant Magnate Caught with His Finger in the Pie.* That was nice, too.

He deserved it. No one could ever argue otherwise. He'd done his best to destroy Sara's career, all because she'd had the audacity to reject his slimy advances. This wouldn't be cruel—it would just be fair.

Benny had come to her because he knew a little about Gavin's history with Sara. Not everything, but enough to know that Gavin had done her wrong. He was also terrified in his own right of what Gavin might do to him if he found out what Benny had discovered. Getting exiled from the business was bad enough. But rumor had it that Gavin had started to run with some rough types lately, and Benny didn't like the thought of a late-night visit from burly men with violent intentions.

Sara thought that that sounded more than a little bit ridiculous. Gavin wasn't exactly a mafioso, after all. But she knew firsthand that the New York City restaurant scene had its fair share of shady characters. Who was to say that Gavin wasn't actually capable of something that nefarious? Gavin would never think to accuse her of disseminating these documents. She was the perfect leak.

So she could do it.

The question was ... should she?

19

MAE

Saoirse and Mae walked down the beach in silence for a while. With the way Saoirse had said *you* in *"I'd like* you *to walk with me,"* Mae thought that maybe the woman had something to tell her. But if so, she wasn't quite ready to spill the beans just yet.

A few minutes of silence was all Mae could bear. It felt like it was suffocating her. "Saoirse, I—"

"What do you know of me?" Saoirse interrupted.

Mae didn't know how to answer that. But that *something* in Saoirse, that reservoir of bittersweet darkness, told her to simply tell the truth for the next few minutes. To see where that current would take them.

"Nothing," she answered simply. It was an honest reply. Two days ago, Mae hadn't even known she existed.

"That is best," Saoirse nodded. "What do you think of me, then?"

Mae tilted her head to the side. "What do you mean?" She'd asked that question far too many times in the last few minutes, and yet here she was, lost in a baffling conversation once again. Saoirse's Irish accent added little eddies and undercurrents of meaning to simple questions. When she said something like *What do you think of me?*, it seemed to carry far more implications than it would if Mae had said the same thing.

She repeated the question. "What do you think of me?"

Mae thought for a moment before answering. "I think I don't know enough to say just yet."

Saoirse just nodded again, like that was a fair answer. Her red-blonde hair caught the evening light and refracted it beautifully amongst her curls. Their shadows stretched ahead of them on the sand, made impossibly long by the angle of the sunset.

The women kept walking. Saoirse spoke up again a few short minutes later. "What do you think of Dominic?"

They'd been strolling for nearly twenty minutes now, long enough that, when Mae glanced back over her shoulder, she could just barely see the dot that was Dominic standing still in the distance. "I think he is a kind man. A thoughtful man."

"Do you think he is a sad man?"

"Sad in what way?"

"Sorrowful."

Round and round in circles they went. Each question begat two more. Mae had half a mind to turn around and end this walk right now. But something made her stay. She wished she knew what that something was.

"I think he can be, yes."

Saoirse came to a sudden halt and pivoted to face Mae directly. At this angle, the sun cast half her face in light and half her face in shadow. It was indescribably beautiful. Her eyes sparkled like wave tops on a clear summer's day.

"He is the saddest man I have ever met in my life," Saoirse declared, as if it was an indisputable fact. "And the saddest man you have ever met in yours. He believes himself to be cursed. Do you know why that is?"

The way her lips pronounced the word *cursed* made Mae feel for the briefest moment like such a thing could even exist in the world. Perhaps it was just a relic of old school fairy tales, but *cursed* passing through the gilding of an Irish accent made it feel as though magic was real, curses were real, all of it was real.

Then she blinked and the moment passed. She realized she was standing on a beach with her boyfriend's ex-wife, talking about curses, and she got very annoyed indeed.

"I must admit," Mae snapped, "I'm a little weary of talking in circles. It has been difficult since you arrived. I'm sorry to be so rude, but it needs to be said. I don't know why he thinks he is cursed and I don't believe in such a childish thing anyhow. Most of all, I don't appreciate being led in endless riddles. Thank you for the invitation to walk, but I'll be taking my leave now."

She had begun to walk away as soon as the words were out of her mouth, but once again, Saoirse's hand clamped down on her forearm. "Mae, stop." She thought about pulling away, but the woman's grip was surprisingly strong.

"I am not here to complicate your life," Saoirse said. "I am here to mourn."

That got Mae's attention. She quirked an eyebrow up and said nothing.

Saoirse studied her face for a long beat before continuing. "Many years ago, when Dominic and I were married, we had a daughter."

A shadow of sadness had passed over Saoirse's face. Her gaze was turned inwards, in a way, like she was seeing something totally different than the beauty of Nantucket around them. She was remembering.

"Her name was Aoife. That means 'joyfully radiant' in Gaelic. She was that; certainly she was." A breeze ran past them. It chilled Mae to the bone. "She was three months old when we lost her. One night with us, the next morning gone. Do you know what that is like?"

"I don't—well. Well, maybe I do. In a way."

"I thought you might," Saoirse said. She kept nodding with that solemn look on her face. Like she knew something about life that Mae hadn't yet learned. "You are not a sorrowful woman, but you have sorrow in you."

Mae stayed quiet. Saoirse had more to say, she could sense.

"She died thirty years ago tomorrow."

Mae started to stammer, "Saoirse, I'm—I'm so sorry—"

"No." Saoirse held up her hand. "It is not your burden to bear. You have enough of those, I think. I do not tell you this to sadden you. Merely to inform you. It is sorrow that brought me here. Nothing more. I hope you sense that I am here for that purpose only."

"Okay," she whispered.

Again, a breeze came rippling down the beach that felt far colder than any June breeze in Nantucket had a right to be. Mae shivered, feeling goose bumps pricking up down her arms, her thighs, the back of her neck. The weight of Saoirse's words and the waltz of her accent combined to give this whole thing an eerie feeling that was totally out of sorts with the sand, the sun, the waves around them.

Mae felt like she was being bewitched. Saoirse had hardly blinked since she'd first stopped Mae from leaving. She had kept her grip on Mae's arm, too. The points of contact where her fingertips met Mae's bare skin seemed to be burning hot. It was like all the rules of the world were broken, and the only thing that held any significant weight anymore was Saoirse's gaze, as blue as the water. Her irises reminded Mae of a vacation that she and Henry had taken once, many years ago. They'd gone down to Belize, and one day they had taken a trip to the site of the Great Blue Hole. One hundred and fifty thousand years ago, it was a cave. Then the sea rose to consume the cave and turned it into a giant sinkhole. The water was so blue there that it hurt Mae's eyes. Henry made a joke about it being "the throat of the ocean." Remembering that harmless joke scared her as much now as it did back then. He wanted to go snorkeling in it. Mae refused. She was scared of being swallowed.

She was scared of being swallowed by Saoirse's gaze, too. There was so much pain in her eyes that Mae shivered once more. The death of her daughter had clearly torn this woman's heart wide open. And as Mae thought back on it, she realized that she could see signs of the same pain in Dominic. He hid it better than Saoirse did. But when he was sitting quietly by himself, when he thought no one was looking at him, there was an agony in his face that Mae had never fully understood.

Now she did.

"Let us go back now," Saoirse said. "I wanted only to tell you why I am here."

"Okay," Mae said again. She didn't know what else to say.

Saoirse's fingertips slid down to linger on Mae's wrist. The women held hands for one long second.

Then Saoirse let go, and they walked back to Dominic, who had not moved.

"Are you ready to go?" he asked them as they approached.

Mae nodded.

"Yes," Saoirse answered. "I am done here."

The three of them turned their backs to the ocean and went walking home through the dunes.

PART III

WHAT THE HEART WANTS

20

OLIVER

Early Friday morning.
One day until the wedding.

∽

It took Oliver eight hours and twenty-six minutes of driving down I-95S to get from Nantucket to the address outside of Philadelphia.

Or rather, that's how long it would've taken, if he hadn't stopped just before New Haven to think about what he was doing. He stopped for nineteen and a half minutes before deciding to turn around and go back home. He drove an hour and twelve minutes back towards Nantucket before stopping and reconsidering a second time. Then he turned towards Philadelphia once more, and finished the drive at a humming fifteen miles per hour over the speed limit.

All said and done, he didn't arrive until the early hours of Friday morning.

He didn't listen to music or the radio the whole trip. All he heard was the rumble of the road under his wheels. One mile at a time, chewing up the distance between him and the man who brought him into this world.

He didn't know what he wanted. He didn't know what was going to happen. He didn't know anything about anything. All he knew was that he had to keep driving.

The early Friday dawn was sticky and gray. Somehow, he didn't feel tired. Thirty-six years of anxiety would do that to a guy, he supposed. Thirty-six years of wondering what kind of man could father him and then leave him. Thirty-six years of endless, unceasing lies, one piled on top of the next like a house of cards until it all came crashing down.

Neal and Marcy had raised Oliver and they'd done the best they knew how to do under the circumstances. That was all fine and well and good. He owed them his thanks, of course. They were good-hearted people. But he wasn't their little boy. He never had been, really. Not because of the biological thing. But because he was a man, in a manner of speaking, from the moment his parents first abandoned him at that—well, wherever they'd abandoned him. The story had shifted over the years. Now, he was beginning to understand why.

Because it was all a lie.

And truth was waiting at #24, 1311 Catfish Lane.

He pulled into a gas station parking lot and stopped. His phone said he had about a half mile to go until he reached his destination. He wanted to take a minute to compose himself before he arrived.

Closing his eyes, he leaned his forehead against the steering wheel. It was warm from his hands squeezing it tightly. He had a pulsing headache behind his temples. *Breathe, idiot,* he told himself. He drew in a shuddering breath, held it for as long as he could, then released it softly, like he was trying to fog a mirror. He could feel his heart rate coming down slowly. But as he flexed his fingertips open and closed, he realized he was shaking.

He couldn't say exactly why. Fear? Hope? Hard to say. Which one was better? Which one was worse? *Let's play out the scenarios,* he thought. He started to do just that—picturing a man who looked just like him opening the door and pulling him into a hug, whispering, *I missed you, my son,* into his ear—before he abruptly jerked his eyes open and pulled his forehead off the steering wheel.

No. Scratch that. No scenarios.

He couldn't control what was going to happen a half mile from now. Screw fear and hope in equal measure. Both were unreliable. He just needed to *know*.

Gripping the car key between thumb and forefinger, he brought the engine sputtering back to life, pulled out, and kept going the rest of the way to Catfish Lane. The road was empty this early. Rush hour would be starting soon, or whatever passed for rush hour out here in the boonies. But for now, silence. Grayness. A light mist hung wreathed amongst the treetops like sad streamers from a party that had long since broken up.

Oliver frowned when he saw the sign for Valley Forge Trailer Park and double-checked the address in his phone. It was right. This was the place.

He turned in. The smooth asphalt of the highway gave way to an unkempt gravel road. Weeds sprouted up between the patches of dirt. He took his foot off the gas pedal and let the car ease down the way. As he passed, he saw window shades flicking open and suspicious eyes following his progress warily.

"Friendly bunch," he muttered. An old man was seated in a lawn chair in front of his mobile home, wearing a wifebeater and a baseball cap pulled low over his eyes. Oliver waved and gritted a smile. The man did nothing but stare back.

When Neal had given him the address at dinner the night before, Oliver had assumed that #24 was an apartment number. He realized now that it was actually a trailer lot number. There were little white signs stuck in each yard, bearing two-digit identifiers in faded black font.

To his left, Oliver saw 19. 21. 23.

He looked right.

20. 22.

There it was.

24.

The trailer looked much the same as the rest of them. Neither the best nor the worst. Probably needed a pressure-wash once-over, or a fresh coat of paint. A pair of foldable camping chairs sat in the front. One was tipped over. Crumpled beer cans studded the ground on all sides.

Oliver swallowed as he steered the car over to the shoulder and put it in park.

One thought was playing in his head incessantly: his father was behind that door.

What was a man supposed to do at a moment like this? A religious man might pray. An angry man might kick the door in. A man like Oliver—a lost man, confused—didn't know what to fall back on. He had neither faith nor rage to chart his path.

So he just got out of his car before he lost his nerve, walked up, and rapped his knuckles lightly on the door.

It didn't make a satisfying knocking sound. The door was too thin and too cheap for that. It popped and crackled, kind of, and wiggled in the frame a little bit. It must be poorly hung.

He held his breath and listened.

The trailer park seemed to be breathing as one. The mist floating around his head felt like a giant's exhale, cool and steamy and somehow gross, all at once. There were crickets, and the occasional creaking of doors opening and then slamming closed. In the distance, a car engine tried and failed to start.

Then, from within—motion.

Oliver heard the sigh of a man, the squeak of a chair as its occupant got up. Footsteps. The inner door wailing as it was forced open.

Then, through the mesh screen, Oliver made eye contact.

It should've been a climactic moment. But it felt as awkward as knocking on any stranger's door at seven in the morning would've been. The man glared, waiting for him to talk. He had dark hair in a messy crew-cut that badly needed a touch-up. His eyes were red-rimmed from lack of sleep, and he was working a plug of chewing tobacco in his lower lip. They were almost exactly the same height, so their eyes locked perfectly level with each other's.

Oliver swallowed. "Are you Jesse Turner?" he rasped when he found his voice.

"Who are you?" the man barked instead of answering the question.

"I'm ... I'm your son. I think."

Surely, the man would react to that. He'd smile, or his eyes would widen, or his jaw would drop.

But none of that happened.

He just kept working at the plug of tobacco. Then he raised the red Solo cup in his hand and unleashed a squelching jet of brown spit into it. "Yeah?" he said finally.

"I think so. That's what I was told, at least."

"And?"

Oliver was at a loss for words. "And I just, uh ... I came to—to find you, I guess."

"I don't have any money for you."

He shook his head. "I don't want any money."

"You a drunk?"

"What? No. I mean, I drink, but—no, not a drunk."

"Churchgoing man?"

"Um. Not really. Lapsed, I guess."

"Good. Can't stand churchy types."

"Uhh ... right."

The man sighed and spit into his cup again. "I s'pose you're wanting to come in, then."

"I guess."

"You guess?"

Oliver was stammering. He had done his level best not to have any expectations for this moment. But this was worse than that, even. This was—what was this? Awful in a way. Cringeworthy, too. Painful and meaningless all at once.

"Yeah," he said finally. "I guess I'll come in."

The man turned and retreated inside without saying another word. He didn't open the door for Oliver. He just walked away.

Oliver hesitated a moment. He thought about how it had sounded in the stillness of the car, the blur of miles disappearing in his rear-view mirror. How the trees had watched him go past on the interstate, stoic and rigid. There had been so much tension in the air. Like a wire on a crank, reeling him in to this finale. Now, everything felt deflated.

Wires snipped. No more pulling. Just loose, dead cord, no purpose left to draw it tight.

He opened the screen door and walked in.

He stopped a few steps in to look around. The place was small and cramped. Not especially dirty, nor especially clean. Some beer cans abandoned in cupholders and some clustered together on the rickety coffee table. Fox News on the television, volume on low. Solo cups everywhere, each with an inch or two of brown tobacco spit in them.

His father—Jesse Turner, according to Neal, a name the man had neither acknowledged nor refuted—was back in his armchair. He lit a cigarette as Oliver stood there and watched him.

"Gonna sit?" the man asked after he'd taken an inhale and released it. The trailer smelled like beer and cigarettes and the pasty, glommed-over stench of too much air freshener.

Oliver sat on the couch across from him.

"Not much of a conversationalist, are you." It wasn't really a question. More like a cruel joke, though it wasn't quite that, either. It was just a thing to say that looked and sounded like everything else around here—gray, flat, unremarkable, vaguely gross.

"I don't know what to say," Oliver whispered by way of reply. It wasn't really an answer. But it was the best he had.

All he knew was that he'd had a powerful, irresistible need to come here. To sit on this cigarette-burned couch and face this man and say —something. Say anything.

He had spoken honestly—he still didn't know what to say. But now that he was here, he knew what he wanted the man to say to him. He wanted his father to say a single word that had love in it. It didn't have to be "I love you," explicitly. That was for Hallmark movies and cheesy books with saccharine endings. It could've just been a hello that didn't sound as callous as everything else the man had said so far. It could've been a "how are you?" that had even an ounce of courtesy in it. Just something that was an acknowledgment from one human to the other. Maybe that was what he'd come searching for. The mere fact of being recognized as kin.

Jesse Turner offered none of that. He just grunted and took another drag on his cigarette.

A million things clamored suddenly at Oliver's throat. "I'm your son," he said. He hated how his voice sounded in this tinny little trailer, bouncing off the walls and mingling with the newscaster on the television.

"You already said that."

"I know."

"Now you've said it twice."

"I guess."

"You're doing a lot of guessing."

"I'm sorry."

"Now you're apologizing? Jesus."

The man grunted again and shook his head like Oliver had disappointed him.

He felt so lost and confused. Okay, yeah, so this wasn't a Hallmark movie. But couldn't the man say something that wasn't a grunt? That didn't feel like the verbal equivalent of stubbing that cigarette out on Oliver's chest. He blinked and looked again at the man and this time he got angry. Bile and rage grew molten hot in his stomach.

"You're supposed to be happy to see me," he said. It sounded like an accusation. Perhaps it was.

His father looked surprised. "Why would I be happy to see you?"

"Because I'm your son."

"That's the third time."

Oliver was up on his feet before he knew it and then his hand was around the man's throat and he was choking him, slamming his head against the back of the armchair, not really doing any actual damage but, God, he wanted to do some so badly. He wanted to hurt this man for abandoning him and for snubbing him at the door and for spitting in all these cups everywhere. That was such a foul and disgusting habit.

Jesse Turner was grunting and trying to pry Oliver's hand off his neck, but Oliver wasn't letting go until *whoompf,* one of his father's fists slammed into Oliver's stomach and knocked the air out of him. He fell to the ground in surprise, knocking his cheekbone against the edge of the coffee table as he went down. He felt his skin give way to the roughshod edge. Blood trickled. When he opened his eyes, he saw his biological father standing over him with his fists balled up and Oliver's handprint already blooming into bruises around the base of his jaw.

"If you don't get out of my house right now," the man he thought was his father growled through clenched teeth, "I'm going to kill you."

Oliver said nothing. His breath was coming hard and fast, so he just laid there while his father glared down at him with pure and vicious hate in his eyes.

"You were supposed to be happy to see me," Oliver whispered. "I'm your son."

"You stopped being my son when I got rid of you."

Silence took over. Absolute and unwavering silence.

Slowly, Oliver got to his feet. Jesse's eyes followed him. The shirt he was wearing had been tugged at the neck during the struggle, so it hung limp and ragged. His teeth were yellowed, Oliver noticed, though still fairly straight.

Oliver backed up towards the door of the trailer. Their eyes never left each other. He got there, reached behind him, felt the handle in his grasp. Something occurred to him before he turned and left.

"What happened to my mother?" he asked in a quiet voice.

Jesse fell back onto the armchair, spat more tobacco juice, and lit another cigarette. He'd broken eye contact, and Oliver could tell immediately that the two of them would never look each other in the eye again.

"Been dead a long time," he answered eventually.

That was the end of it.

There were many things Oliver could have thought about as he got back into his car and exited Valley Forge Trailer Park. He remembered a line from a sitcom about wishing there was a way to know that you were in the good ol' days before the good ol' days were over. The way he was feeling now was the exact opposite. He knew, firmly and irrevocably, that he was walking away from a moment that would forever define the rest of his life. It was like standing up from a plane crash somehow completely unscathed and realizing that you would never, ever fly again. He had left part of himself in that trailer. He wouldn't be getting it back.

But of all the things that Oliver could be thinking of as the road merged onto the highway, he found himself thinking about his job interview next week. It was the culmination of a year-long search done half-heartedly, mostly late at night or early in the morning, when Eliza and Winter were sleeping. He felt as he sat at the computer, combing through job postings, that he was betraying himself in a way. Giving up on music meant giving up on the only thing that had never given up on him.

He closed his eyes and pictured wearing a tie. He pictured answering to a boss. He pictured boring meetings and acronyms and tepid coffee in paper cups. He'd spent two decades imagining those things as proof positive of failure. If he ended up in an office, it was because he quit on the only thing that mattered.

He didn't feel that way anymore.

As he drove away, car aimed back towards Nantucket, he shed a skin, in a way. He was leaving one question behind and picking up another. He was picking up a million questions, actually. He was picking up "Can you help me, Daddy?" and "Do you love me, husband?" and "Can you protect your girls forever?"

The question he was leaving behind was, "Why did you abandon me?"

He hadn't known that he'd wanted an answer to that. But he knew— suddenly, permanently—that he'd in fact wanted an answer to that forever.

Until he didn't.

He called Eliza. She answered on the second ring, though it was still early in the morning and she was probably hoping to keep sleeping as long as Winter did. "Babe?" she asked.

"I love you," he said. "I'm on my way home. I just wanted you to know."

She hesitated. He knew she was biting her lip, trying to hold back the tide of questions he was sure she wanted to ask. But she didn't ask any of them. She just exhaled and said, "I love you too, Oliver. I can't wait to see you."

He squeezed the steering wheel tightly. His family was in Nantucket. Everything behind him no longer mattered.

21

BRENT

Henrietta slept through the night. Brent didn't, not really. He woke up every hour to check her breathing, holding a hand in front of her nose to feel the puffs of inhale, exhale, inhale, exhale. Dawn came and went. The sun peered through the slats in the blinds and prodded him in the eyeballs.

The sharp pang of worry ebbed away bit by bit, though he still felt that dull ache in his gut that he was learning to recognize as a kind of love and concern that wouldn't ever leave him. Henrietta would be okay, he could tell. That was a good thing.

Marshall texted him to check in. *How's the pup, amigo?*

Steady as she goes. She'll still outrun you, even now.

I don't doubt it, he wrote back. *Back to the vet today?*

Yeah. Just wanna be sure things are fine.

When you going?

Soon.

I'll come scoop you. Make me some coffee.

Twenty minutes later, the two of them were in Marshall's truck, headed towards the vet's office. Henrietta had woken up, though the last of the sedative in her system kept her moored in a calm mood. She rested her chin on the car door and hung her nose out the window as they drove down the road.

Pulling to a halt in the parking lot of the office, Brent went around and helped his dog down to the ground. She was walking gingerly, kind of waddling almost. She looked a little bloated, too. Brent wondered if she was plumper than normal or if he was just imagining things. He made a mental note to ask the doctor to check her weight chart. He couldn't remember off-hand what she normally weighed, but he could swear she'd packed on a few pounds of late.

They made their way into the small office. It smelled like animals in here, that sort of dirty funkiness of fur mingling with the blasé glaze of disinfectant. Dr. Dawson came out from the examination room to greet them. She looked the way she did yesterday: competent, professional. The kind of person you call in an emergency when you're freaking out and you need someone who can still do things with a steady hand. Those were good qualities in a vet, Brent thought.

"Good morning!" Dr. Dawson greeted as they entered.

Brent was halfway to replying when Marshall butted in. "Morning, Doc," he said with a wry smile and a tip of an imaginary hat. "Fancy seeing you here." Brent could've sworn that Marshall was doing a horrible cowboy accent. It was awfully early for Marshall's antics, but he knew better than to try and dissuade the guy. That usually only made things worse.

"Didn't think *you* would be back quite so soon," she answered, tilting her head to single out Marshall.

"Well, a pal needed my help, so I just thought—"

"— *You* called me and *offered* to drive, champ," Brent butted in.

Marshall shushed him. "Simmer down, sport, the grown-ups are talking."

"Please excuse my friend here," Brent said to the vet, rolling his eyes. "He has a disease that prevents him from ever shutting up."

"Maybe I oughta take a look at that." She winked.

Brent groaned. Dr. Dawson was no help whatsoever. He could practically feel Marshall beaming at his side at the prospect of someone buying into his charm.

"Maybe you oughta indeed." Marshall grinned.

"Doc, he's beyond help, I promise you."

"She's got a duty to aid those in need, Triple B. Hippocratic Oath. Maybe *you* oughta go read a book or something while I get checked out."

"Do vets even take that oath?" Brent asked. "Actually, never mind. We're getting side-tracked here. I brought Henrietta back to see you."

"Early birds," Dr. Dawson commented with a half-smile.

"Well, I didn't get much in the way of sleep," Brent said. "She did all right, though. Seemed comfortable enough, for whatever that's worth."

"Good," Dr. Dawson said, nodding. "Let's get her back here and up on the table so I can take a look at everything." She glanced back over to Marshall and smiled again. "We'll get to you next, Mr. Cook."

Marshall tipped that invisible hat again and settled down into one of the seats in the waiting area.

"C'mon, girl," Brent said, looking down at Henrietta. She whined back at him, a kind of throaty growl he almost never heard from her. But she followed him dutifully as the three of them went into the vet's office. They left Marshall behind with a massive, goofy smile still glowing on his face.

"Right up here, Mr. Benson," Dr. Dawson said. She patted the cold metallic tabletop. Brent bent down to pick her up, but when he looped a hand beneath her belly, she yelped loudly. He recoiled and looked at her oddly.

"What's going on with you, darling?" he murmured to her. He felt Dr. Dawson's eyes on him. He knew he was good to Henrietta, that she had a good life with him, but he still felt like there was maybe a chance that she was judging him. She hadn't done or said anything to make him think that. Just one of those sneaking feelings where he was racking his brain to make sure he'd crossed his t's and dotted his i's when it came to canine care. Like how, when you ask someone with help for something, you wanna be darn sure that you've checked all the right things before the backup arrives.

She didn't say anything, though. So, bending over once more, he grabbed Henrietta with a different hold and hefted her up carefully. She didn't yelp this time, though she did lick her chops in what Brent thought was a kind of uncomfortable fashion. Maybe he was just reading too much into things now.

Dr. Dawson took over once Brent stepped back out of the way. He watched her hands glide delicately over Henrietta's snout, her legs, her belly. Her fingertips were probing, but in the gentlest way. There was a lot of care and love in that touch. He could feel it coming off her like heat waves. It helped to settle his own stomach a little bit, to beat back the last vestiges of the worry that had kept him up all night long.

"Think she's looking all right?" he asked as Dr. Dawson continued her examination.

"Nothing that's alarming me right away, but I do want to run a couple tests. I hate to kick you out, but it'd make my job a little easier if I could have the room to myself."

"Oh, that's all right," he said, nodding. His dog was in good hands. It was okay to be a few feet away, just over there in the waiting room.

That was what he told himself. He closed his eyes and pictured Rose touching his forearm, her honey-gold eyes absorbing him, her saying, *Brent, baby—breathe.* He exhaled and let the anxiety ripple out with his breath. "I'll just go wait with Marsh then."

Dr. Dawson nodded and shut the door behind him after he'd stepped through.

"How's our prized pooch looking?" Marshall asked. Brent settled into the seat next to him. His foot was tapping erratically on the ground. He felt Marshall eye him and note the remaining nervousness, but thankfully, his friend said nothing.

"She's a good doc, I think," Brent replied.

"Yeah," agreed Marshall. "I think so too."

They fell silent for a couple minutes. There wasn't much noise coming out of the exam room. Just intermittent footsteps, the shuffling of papers and metal equipment, the electronic beep of a monitor. Brent tried not to think too much about it. She was going to be fine, the doc had said. He had no reason to doubt her.

"You know something," Brent said after a while, "we never had pets growing up. Not even one. Isn't that the strangest thing? Dad of all people was against it. You'd have thought that he would be the first guy to take in a stray or whatever. He loved other people's pets. But we weren't allowed to have any. Not even a fish."

"Why's that?"

"I think that he just couldn't bear the thought of an animal being trapped inside. Or of anything being trapped inside, come to think of it. He loved his freedom so much. Hated when Mom tried to put him on a schedule or told him where to be. And if he hated it, he figured everything and everyone else hated it, too."

"How do you square that with fishing?"

Brent laughed and scratched the back of his head. "Fair point. Maybe Dad's philosophies weren't always one hundred percent thought through."

"Heart was in the right place, though."

"That it was. But you know the craziest thing about all that? It means Henrietta is basically the first living thing to ever trust me to take care of them."

Marshall chuckled low and said, "And here you had me thinking she was a smart dog. Guess not."

Brent slugged him in the shoulder, but he was laughing too. "Smarter than you."

Marshall raised his hands in admission. "If I was half as smart as that dog, I'd be doing just fine."

"She's a good one."

"Yeah, man. She is. She's gonna be all right, too."

"You think so?" Brent didn't mean for the question to sound so hopeful and uncertain coming out of his lips. He sounded like a little kid looking to his parent for confidence in an outcome that was still far from decided.

But for his part, Marshall didn't seem to acknowledge that. Or if he did, he didn't show it. He just gripped Brent by the shoulder, looked him square in the eye, and said, "Yeah, man. She's gonna be just fine."

Brent hadn't realized how much he'd needed an answer like that.

He had a flashback to elementary school, or maybe it was early in middle school. He couldn't remember. But whenever it was, he'd been assigned a project of growing tomato plants under different conditions—lots of water, little water, salty water, lots of sun, little sun, on and on like that—and seeing which did best. His classmates had all come back at the end of the semester with at least a few of their plants flourishing. Some even had little budding tomatoes weighing down the branches.

All Brent had to show was barren soil.

It wasn't that he thought he was cursed or anything like that. He was just a black thumb, he figured. Not much use for caring for things.

But, out of nowhere, he'd stumbled into a season of his life where caring for things was starting to matter more and more.

You were great with the kids today.

That implied question was still swimming in the back of his head. It wasn't even a fully formed question, actually. More like a raw hope. Like the seed of a question, still nestled underneath the soil. Light and water and time might make it grow into something that had shape, substance. Not yet, but soon, he'd have to have an answer.

So, when Marshall squeezed his shoulder and looked him in the eye and said, *"Yeah, man; She's going to be just fine"*—well, it felt like maybe he'd be able to look Rose in the eyes one day and answer the question that she wanted to ask but didn't dare put to words yet. It felt like maybe that seed was growing.

The door to the exam room creaked open again, interrupting his thoughts. Dr. Dawson ushered him in. She had a cryptic smile on her face that confused him. It didn't look like a bearer-of-bad-news smile. What could it be?

Henrietta looked up at him and whined when he entered. "Hey, babe," he said, petting her where she liked on the chest. She was lying on her side. From this angle, she looked even heavier than she had when they were walking in. That, plus the ultrasound device still lying on the table where Dr. Dawson had set it down, clicked together at once.

He looked up at the veterinarian and his jaw dropped.

"She's pregnant," he said.

Dr. Dawson smiled bigger.

"So what're you gonna do with all those puppies?" Marshall asked as they neared Rose's house. All of Henrietta's stuff was still there since they'd spent the night, so he was going to go collect it all before heading back to his apartment.

"That's a good question," Brent said. He was still a little taken aback by Dr. Dawson's discovery. Henrietta being pregnant explained so much, though. He still didn't know how he'd missed the signs. It was so obvious in retrospect. Sleeping and eating at weird times and in weird amounts, growling at Susanna, the weight gain. He should've known. He felt a little guilty for not recognizing it, but that paled in the face of having a perfectly normal explanation for her behavior. Between that and getting the all-clear on any lingering effects of the snakebite, Brent was super relieved.

But Marshall's question remained: what would he do with the puppies? He'd have to figure that out when the time came, he supposed. Not much he could do about the situation right now, after all.

Marshall dropped him off out front and waved goodbye. Brent ducked inside real quick to gather up Henrietta's and his things, then piled it all in the back seat of his truck. He helped Henrietta into the front seat and headed out. He had a few things to take care of at a couple of his work sites, so he'd have to drop her off at his place and leave her alone for a few hours, though he didn't much love that idea.

It occurred to him as he packed up the car and put the key into the ignition that he wouldn't be doing this two-home thing for much longer. He spent most nights with Rose now, but as with everything else in their tender new relationship, they'd decided to take it slow. This step of moving in together felt momentous.

And it wasn't just that they were moving in together. They were moving in together into a house, one that Brent was in the process of buying. The house he had grown up in, no less! His own father had built the thing with his own two hands. That filled Brent with the strangest blend of pride and longing. He wished, not for the first time, that his dad was around to see him turn this corner in his life. He'd be proud.

Brent's head and heart were full as he pulled out of the driveway, one hand on the steering wheel and the other resting gently on Henrietta's back where she sat riding shotgun next to him. He stopped just before leaving when he noticed something sticking out of the mailbox. Weird—they never got mail here. He hopped out to grab whatever it was. Probably some junk.

But when he got back into his vehicle and looked at it, he froze. It wasn't junk, not at all. It was a postcard from Bali, Indonesia. The front showed a massive rock outcropping sticking out into the bluest ocean water he'd ever seen. It looked like a dolphin made of stone that had been frozen halfway into its dive. Green grasses clung to the top and side, giving way to gray granite just before the water took over. The whole scene was otherworldly. So much color, so much vibrancy. He turned it over, smiling softly, and saw exactly what he expected to see.

Brent, it began in a loopy scrawl. *It's a big world. Bigger than even I thought, as it turns out. There are so many beautiful corners of it. You really do need to come see them all one day.*

I found my corner, though, I think. The water here is so blue. Bluer than Nantucket, even. And it's warm all the time and there are coconuts to drink on the beach and the locals all smile and wave whenever you walk past.

I found someone to share my corner with, too. He's nice. You'd like him. I do. We're getting married soon. Barefoot on the beach, and then I'm gonna run into the water in my dress, just like I did that night with you last summer.

I just wanted to you to know that I'm happy. I hope you are, too.

With love and affection,

Ally

Brent smiled and looked up into the sky. If she was in Bali, that meant that she was pretty much on the exact opposite side of the earth. It'd be night there right now. He wondered if she was looking up at the sky. If she was, then the sun he was seeing now was bouncing its light off the moon. So they were sharing that, in a roundabout way. That made him happy for reasons he couldn't quite explain.

Everything worked out for everyone. She had a man and she was going to get married on the beach with bare feet. That was perfectly Ally.

He had a woman and they were going to move into the house his father had built. That was perfectly him.

Good for her. Good for him. Good for them.

22

ELIZA

Eliza fell back asleep after Oliver called. She'd been worried sick about him, of course. She knew that he had gone on a mission that lived somewhere in a dark, sealed box in his heart that he never opened for anyone, not even himself. She couldn't pretend to know what it was like to be him. His struggles were about family, manhood, his place in the world. She, on the other hand, had been born rich with family. She had siblings who looked up to her, parents who loved her. She knew her place in the world.

Or at least, she used to.

She'd spent the last two years learning that maybe the things she thought about herself weren't always true. That maybe it was just a story she'd told herself or that other people had told her. *Golden Girl Eliza. Perfect Child Eliza. Eliza the Chosen One.* Sara was responsible for the bulk of those nicknames, but Eliza knew that pretty much everyone she crossed paths with shared the same sentiments as her sister. People thought her life was easy. For a long time, it had been.

But things were harder now.

Maybe she just used up all her luck in her first three decades. Because it sure felt like she was getting horribly unlucky lately. First, the storm, now Oliver's departure. Both things left her feeling the same way: completely and utterly helpless.

What was she supposed to do to stop a hurricane? She couldn't exactly go down to the beach and scream at the oncoming clouds to go away please. What she told herself was that the storm's arrival still wasn't a sure thing. Some indicators said it might stall offshore instead of sweeping through Nantucket tomorrow. But as much as she wanted to believe in those predictions, she knew that getting herself hopeful and then suffering the crash if the storm came anyway would be way worse. So she just chewed her nails and fretted.

That was pretty much the same approach she took with Oliver, too. She had slept most of the night—as would any sleep-deprived mother of a young child, no matter the circumstances—but she'd woken up at the stroke of midnight feeling like there was a giant, invisible vise squeezing the air out of her lungs. When she reached over to Oliver's side of the bed for comfort, she found it cold and remembered that she was alone. It was a nasty shock for someone already on edge. It took her a long time to fall back asleep after that.

But eventually, she had. Until her phone started buzzing a little after seven in the morning. She'd slept with it in her hand just in case Oliver called. She hadn't really expected him to call, though. Truth be told, she didn't know what to expect. This wasn't exactly the kind of errand that fit into a neat little box. This was a man going to find the father he never knew still existed. Who could say how long that would take?

Less than a day, apparently. Oliver sounded tense on the phone. She knew at once that something bad had happened. But she knew she shouldn't ask him just yet, either. There would be a time and a place for that, when he was back home in her arms. Now wasn't the right moment.

Still, when they hung up after exchanging I love yous, she was wide awake. Winter was still sleeping and probably would be for a little longer. Eliza thought about checking the weather reports, but she decided against it. No news was better than bad news. She couldn't handle another blow right now. Better to just start some coffee and ease into her day.

But as she took to her feet and put her feet into her slippers, she got rocked with a sudden wave of nausea. Fortunately, it was only a few quick steps to the bathroom. If it was much farther, she wouldn't have made it. She reached the toilet, collapsed, and vomited until her stomach was empty.

When she'd finished hurling up last night's dinner, she sank to her knees on the tiled floor. She knew with a sudden and shocking certainty that she was pregnant again.

Her mind flashed back to the last time she'd been in this position. It was so much like this, and yet so different. Both times, she'd been floored by morning sickness. Both times, she'd realized before she was even done vomiting what the cause was.

But this time, there was love to catch her. Not like before, when she'd been alone in the bathroom of the Goldman Sachs office, ensnared in a life and relationship she hated. It wasn't anything to be feared now. It was something to be celebrated.

A baby. With Oliver.

She stood up to brush her teeth and smiled when she caught sight of herself in the mirror. "Let the storm come," she whispered to her reflection. "This time, I'm ready."

23

MAE

Friday at dawn.

〜

Mae dreamt that night of an empty crib. Red ambulance lights piercing through the curtains. Muffled crying. She saw, clear as day, the nested blanket that had just been warm with the body of an infant. Whether it was just a dream or some kind of vision, she would never be sure. All she knew when she woke up was that her heart ached.

It ached like it had ached when she first saw Brent standing on her doorstep in the rain two years ago, come to tell her that her Henry was dead. This was a twin ache to that. Similar and yet distinct. A riff on the same theme.

When she forced her eyes open and sat up in bed, she knew that she, Dominic, and Saoirse were forever linked by that pain. She didn't have to like Saoirse. In fact, she was certain that she did not like the woman at all. But that wasn't the point. The point was that there was a steel cord tethering them together. The steel cord of pain.

Unimaginable loss. They could merely look at each other and recognize the signs of weariness in the other. After an event like that —the loss of a husband, of a child—gravity seemed to pull a person more heavily towards the ground. No matter how many days passed, the extra weight would never leave. You just had to hope that you were strong enough to bear the load.

That was grieving. That was loss. That was life.

Mae saw all those truths in Saoirse's eyes on the beach. In some ways, it made her own burden feel heavier. It reminded her of the moment it was first dropped on her shoulders. So unexpected, so harsh, so sudden. She had done her best to forget about that night in the days and weeks since. But the sadness that emanated from Saoirse was impossible to ignore or to forget. It was Mae's own sadness, reflected in another person.

In another way, though, it made Mae's burden feel lighter. She wasn't the only one who had been cut down by grief. There was someone else out there who knew what Mae knew. She could look at Saoirse— this woman she didn't know, this intruder, this threat to the fragile domestic happiness she'd cobbled together for herself in the wake of tragedy—and she could hate her. But that would be missing the point. In her, Mae had found someone who understood. Saoirse didn't just understand how it felt to lose a loved one. People all around the world lost loved ones every single day. That was part of life. No, Saoirse understood *everything.* She understood what Mae felt when she looked in the mirror and saw an older woman who refused to give up on life. She understood how it felt to bring a child into this world and to love and be loved so intensely by a good man.

So, try as she might, it was impossible to hate Saoirse. Mae was Saoirse and Saoirse was Mae. Different nationalities, different experiences, different women altogether.

And yet, in all the ways that mattered, they were the same.

Those were the thoughts that rushed into Mae's head when she woke up from her dream in the still-dark hours of Friday morning. They were all there at once, like she'd just brushed off some dirt and found them buried intact below the surface. Dinosaur bones. Ancient truths. It was a bit disconcerting to think that there were all these things she felt that she hadn't even been aware of. What else was lying down there, waiting to be unearthed? Who could say?

She tried to go back to sleep after that. But the bed was empty and the room was dark. For some reason, that unsettled her. Dominic had disappeared into his writing nook as soon as the three of them returned from the beach. Mae had heard him typing long into the night, and he hadn't come to bed.

Until now.

She looked up at that exact moment and saw him standing in the doorway. He froze when he saw that she was awake. They gazed back at each other, or at least in that general direction. It was too dark to tell exactly where his eyes were. Mae wondered, not for the first time, what he was thinking about. So many things happening in that man's mind. More than she'd ever suspected.

It made her wonder what it meant to truly know a person. Why did she feel like she *knew* Saoirse, this woman who'd been in her world for less than a few days? And why did she feel like this man, with whom she'd shared a home and a bed and a life for almost two years ... why did she feel like he was such a locked box of secrets? Would he always feel that way? Could she accept that reality?

"You should be asleep," he said.

"As should you."

He sighed and stepped forward into the beam of moonlight that had penetrated through the skylight set high in the wall behind the bed. She watched as he took his glasses off, closed his eyes, and rubbed the bridge of his nose like a migraine was wreaking havoc on his skull. "I had to write." He settled his glasses back on and looked at her again. "The words were yelling at me."

She saw that he was trying to smile at her, but it looked more like a grimace. She nodded solemnly.

The truth was that she was still mad at him. She'd always be a little mad at him after this week, she thought. He'd permanently stained what was supposed to be a happy week in her life. She wouldn't ever be able to look back on her eldest daughter's wedding without thinking of Saoirse, of the irritation her arrival brought. And also of the pain she revealed in Dominic.

But she also had that urge in her soul to reach out and comfort him. Maybe it was because she was a mother. Maybe it was because she was a nurturer by nature. Maybe it was because, now that Saoirse had pointed it out, she could see how profoundly sad her boyfriend was. She wanted to pull his head into her lap and stroke his hair until he sighed and fell asleep. She wanted to hold his hand or make him laugh or cook him a midnight treat, if only to see a slight smile cross his face.

It should be impossible to feel this many things at once, she thought. Anger and sorrow and anxiety and the powerful need to make things right in the life of another person. How could one person hold all these feelings inside at the same time?

She had always coped by staying busy. But right here, in this dark and silent bedroom, with the saddest man in the world standing in a shaft of moonlight and sighing because he had a throbbing headache and a broken heart, there was nothing to do to occupy her mind. She had to face her feelings. She couldn't run.

"What did the words tell you?" she asked softly.

"What they always tell me," he answered. "Everything and nothing at the same time."

"Did you write about her?"

"Aoife."

"Yes."

He sighed again, long, pained, and slow. "Yes," he answered finally. "I wrote about her."

Mae nodded again. "Do you want to come to bed?" she asked.

Dominic looked at her. His eyes were sparkling behind his glasses, refracting the moonlight in their depths. Eventually, he nodded back. "I would like that."

She patted the mattress next to her. Dominic undressed and slid under the comforter next to her. She pulled his head into her lap and leaned back against the pillows. One hand ran through his hair over and over, teasing through the curls. He held the other hand and stroked the back of her knuckles.

Neither of them said a word. When the sun came up, it found them sleeping together, breathing in rhythm, hands still intertwined. Nothing had been said, but nothing had to be said, either.

Everything they needed was right here.

PART IV

THE BIG DAY

24

HOLLY

Saturday morning.
Eliza's wedding day.

The day was finally here.

Holly was giddy. She'd been looking forward to Eliza's wedding ever since she first heard the news. Oliver and Eliza had video called her when they landed in Bermuda. That had been a doozy of a conversation! "Hey, we quit the tour, we're in Bermuda, and oh by the way, we're getting married." Eliza never did anything halfway, but still —that was certainly a lot to take in all at once.

It sure seemed like the right decision, though. Eliza was so happy these days. That was a good thing. She deserved it.

Holly sent Eliza a quick text first thing upon waking up. Just a little "Hi, I love you, can't wait for today. XO." She knew Eliza would be bubbly and nervous and excited.

Especially due to the news they'd gotten last night: an unexpected cold front had emerged virtually out of nowhere and stalled the hurricane offshore. Nantucket was safe, at least for a little bit longer. Pete had come bouncing into the room the night before to tell Holly about the latest update.

"You gotta be kidding me!" Holly exclaimed.

"Nope," he replied. "Just sitting out over the ocean like it knew it wasn't invited to the party."

Holly let out a long sigh. She didn't know whether to be relieved or furious at the storm for causing so much chaos, only to amount to a whole bunch of nothing in the end.

She barely slept. She had those little-kid jitters, like how she used to feel before the first day of a new school year. Pretty much every hour on the hour, she woke up and glanced over at the clock, hoping it was time to get up and get started.

Finally, at long last, someone in the heavens above took pity on her and fast-forwarded the hours until it was a little before seven. "Good enough," she mumbled to herself. Pete made a grunting noise over on his side of the bed. She poked him in the side. "Gotta get up soon," she said. "Big day ahead."

"Mmhmmf."

Holly laughed and went off to shower. Her husband wasn't particularly fond of early wake-up calls, no matter the occasion.

But on a day like today, how could you not just spring out of bed, bright-eyed and bushy-tailed? Okay, maybe she was being a little ridiculous, but it was her older sister's wedding. *Someone* ought to be visibly excited.

By the time she emerged from the shower, Pete was sitting in bed with a cup of coffee at his side. He looked over at her and smiled.

"Aren't you a sight for sore eyes?" he teased.

Holly glanced at herself in the mirror. She was fresh-faced, wearing a bathrobe and a towel wrapped around her hair. Not exactly runway-ready. But it was a cute sentiment anyway. "You better get moving, bucko," she chided. "It's gonna take us half an hour at least to get Grady all dolled up."

Pete looked at her with horror in his eyes. "Don't tell me we didn't get him a clip-on tie."

Holly chuckled and shook her head. "He got the real deal, same as you."

"Oh jeez," Pete mumbled, looking into the distance like a soldier preparing for war. "That's gonna be a nightmare."

"I figure it'll be some nice father-son bonding time."

"Yeah, well, if he puts up a fight, I'm just gonna tie the tie reaaaal tight."

"Pete Goodwin!" Holly snapped, though she was laughing as she whacked him over the head with a pillow. "That's our firstborn son you're threatening."

He ducked her follow-up blow, slipped out from under the comforter, and sidled over to the bathroom, calling over his shoulder as he went, "Then he better cooperate, if he knows what's good for him!"

Holly laughed once more as her husband stepped into the shower. It was time to wake up the kids and get the two of them mobilized. Then she had to throw on a quick outfit and go over to Eliza's bridal suite to finish getting ready with the rest of the girls.

She padded into Grady's room first. He moaned something about waking up early on a Saturday, and the first Saturday of summer break, no less! He'd always been a sleeper, that one; Holly had a feeling he was going to test her limits as they ventured into his teen years. When she was confident that he was up and at 'em, she went through the Jack & Jill bathroom into her daughter's room. Alice was a little reticent to get up, too. But there was no obstacle too large for Holly to tackle today, and to tackle with a smile on her face no less. She just kept saying, "Up! Up! Up!" in an obnoxiously sing-songy voice until both of her children were awake and grimacing at her.

She hustled Alice into the shower while she got Grady set up with a bowl of cereal for breakfast. Then, when she was satisfied that they could operate self-sufficiently for the next few minutes, she laid out their clothes on their beds and returned to her bedroom to pack everything she would need for the morning.

Pete was shaving and singing to himself in the mirror, some low old crooner's song. She peeked through the crack in the bathroom door and watched him. Her heart swelled with love. He had a towel tied around his waist and no shirt on. His skin was a little bit flushed from the heat of the shower and he really ought to spend a little more time in the sun to do something about that pastiness. But she loved watching his shoulders and forearms flex and move as he turned this way and that. She loved how capable his hands looked—strong, deft, nimble. She closed her eyes and inhaled deeply as he applied cologne, loving how it mingled with the remnant steam of the shower and the soap Pete favored. He was hers, hers, hers. She loved him. She loved all of him.

Shyly, she pulled the door open a touch more and slipped through, then walked up behind Pete and laid her cheek between his shoulder blades. Her hands hugged around his waist. He stopped, surprised, and laughed.

"Sneaking up on me now, are ya?" he accused with a grin.

"Shh," she admonished, keeping her eyes closed. She took another deep inhale of his scent—that spicy, woodsy cologne, the cleanliness of the shaving cream, and that innately Pete smell—and let it fill her. "Just let me hug my husband and be happy for a second."

He opened his mouth to say something else witty, then thought better of it and patted her hand where it clung to his stomach.

They stood there for a minute, maybe more, as curls of steam rose and fell around them and the coolness of the air conditioning snuck through the cracked-open door to nip away at the remaining heat. The contrast of the two temperatures played against Holly's skin. Her nose was filled with scents. Her face, still lying against her husband's back, was soft and relaxed. It felt like they were floating in a cloud together.

"Do you remember our wedding?" Pete asked softly.

"No," Holly teased, sliding her chin up to rest on Pete's shoulder so she could look at their reflection in the mirror. "Tell me about it."

"You kept laughing during the vows."

"I did not!"

"You did too. You held it back good, but I saw right through you. Giggle fits."

"You're making things up now."

"I would never."

"Well," Holly said, "I remember that you tried to smear some icing on my face and you got it in my hair instead."

"You flinched!"

"*I would never,*" she mimicked in his voice.

Pete wagged his razor threateningly at their reflection. She'd moved her head so her chin rested on his shoulder and they were both looking at each other in the mirror, smiling. "Watch yourself, Benson," he warned.

"I'm a Goodwin now," Holly said in a quiet voice. "All yours."

He couldn't help but smile at that. He turned around and settled his hands on Holly's waist, then leaned his forehead over to rest against hers. His glistening eyes, his sweet breath, the warmth and breadth of his love—all of it took up Holly's vision. Pete was all that she could hear or smell or sense. She felt wrapped up in him, consumed by him. She felt safe and loved here.

"That's right," he murmured. She watched his lips move. "And I'm all yours."

"That's right," she repeated.

It felt, in the strangest way, like taking vows of their own again. Like recommitting to each other. So when she tilted her chin up and kissed Pete softly on the lips, that too felt like a reenactment of their own wedding. Full circle, both here now and back then at the same time, all of it linking up until that surrounded her too, just like the steam and the scent and Pete's love. She felt blissfully, deliriously happy.

Pete's cell phone began to vibrate where it sat on the countertop. Sighing, he broke apart their kiss and glanced down at it. When he saw the caller ID, he rolled his eyes. "World's most annoying client," he bemoaned.

Holly smiled up at him. "Take it," she said. "I'll go finish getting the kids ready."

"You sure?" His eyes searched hers. He knew darn well the rules they'd set up about when work could and could not intrude on their lives. But right now, it didn't matter. Right now, Pete could do no wrong. He loved her. In so many ways, that was the only thing she needed.

"Positive," she said. She leaned up and kissed him once more. Then she pinched his bottom and scampered out before he could get her back, the two of them giggling like they really were newlyweds.

She stepped out of the bathroom and back into the coolness of the bedroom. But the feeling of being surrounded by warm love never left her. Maybe it never would.

25

SARA

Sara had been wrestling with her secrets for two straight days and nights.

As she sat in Eliza's bridal room while the hairdresser braided her hair, she stared into the distance and let her mind wander back and forth over the same question it had been considering since Benny first emailed her: what should she do?

She was no closer to an answer than she had been in that very first moment of opening the email. She felt rage and guilt in equal measure. Neither one was convincing enough to make her act one way or the other.

She didn't know what she was waiting for. Some sign from the universe? It's not like an angel was going to beam down from the heavens above and reveal to her what she should do with the information she had. She wasn't going to go to the library and find a how-to manual on destroying a person's reputation. That wouldn't help, anyway. What she needed was a "whether-to-do manual." The "how" of it was simple: Call a reporter. Explain the scoop. Forward the documents. Then sit back and watch the fireworks. It was the "if" that was keeping her up at night.

This wasn't the time or the place to be considering these questions, either. It was supposed to be a happy day, a joyous day, right? Eliza was getting married! Holly had been blowing up the Benson girls' group text message thread all morning with googly eyes and heart emojis. That was typical Holly, of course—a notorious sap if ever there was one. But Sara ought to be joining in.

She looked around the room. It was a happy room for a happy day. The windows set high in the walls were allowing that pearly early-morning Nantucket sunlight to shine through and cast everything in a soft white glow. The mirrors reflected the light, too, doubling it and tripling it until it felt like they were seated in the middle of a star. There were lilacs in vases set on every flat surface, the same color as the bridesmaid robe that Sara was wearing with her name embroidered in royal purple thread on the breast pocket. A fan whirred lazily overhead, and gentle music played through a speaker set up in one corner. This was a happy place, to be sure.

Sara knew that Eliza deserved happiness. After everything she'd been through, she deserved at least one day of carefree bliss. It was just hard for Sara to pretend her heart was in it right now.

Right then, as if she was reading her brain, Eliza turned to Sara. "What's on your mind?" she asked.

Sara forced a smile. "Not a thing."

"Liar."

"That's rude."

"Not if I'm right."

"You're not."

"Again—liar."

Sara sighed. "It's your big day. We don't need to worry about my problems right now."

Eliza turned to the hairdresser duo who were working on the two of them. "I'm really sorry, but do you ladies mind giving us just one sec?"

"No, no, no—" Sara started to say, but Eliza pinched her thigh until she yelped "Ouch!" instead. The hairdressers smiled and ducked out immediately, leaving just Sara and Eliza alone in the room. Holly would be here shortly, as soon as she got Pete and the kids taken care of, and Mom would be coming by in a little bit as well. But for now, it was just the two of them.

"All right," Eliza said, turning to face Sara again. She leaned forward to grab Sara's hands in hers and fixed her with a serious gaze, that big sister look that Eliza had perfected decades ago. "Talk to me."

"It's really not important," protested Sara, but she hardly had the words out of her mouth before Eliza shook her head firmly.

"Talk to me," she repeated. Demanded. "It's definitely important, and I want to hear about it. Besides, it's my wedding day. I get what I want."

"I think you have that confused with your birthday," Sara joked lamely. Eliza pinched her on the thigh a second time and Sara yelped once more. "Fine," she groaned. "I ... I don't know where to start."

Eliza didn't hesitate. "The beginning."

So that was what Sara did. She told Eliza about the email, about her battle with revenge versus forgiveness, about how she didn't know what to do next. Eliza held her hands and listened intently, as if this was the only thing in the world that mattered right now.

Sara felt so guilty. She meant what she had said—this wasn't important, not right now, not today. Eliza was getting married. Surely Sara's problems could wait.

But Eliza was as stubborn as Sara was, and she knew that her eldest sister was every bit as serious about listening as she was about everything else in her life. New Eliza might have relaxed somewhat compared to Old Eliza, but she could still turn up the intensity meter when she wanted to. It was on full blast at the moment.

When she finished telling the story, Eliza was silent. She sat back and let one of Sara's hands go, though she still kept a tight grasp on the other. She glanced out the window like there was an answer written there. Sara followed her gaze. From here, they could see just a sliver of the beach. The waves were rolling in strong, thanks to the hurricane offshore. The whitecaps were thick and expressive, like eyebrows on the face of the ocean.

Sara remembered thinking that the ocean was alive when she was younger. Like an entity, a being in its own right. That, like so many other little kid beliefs, faded away over time. But she never lost the sense of seeing moods in the waves. Right now, she thought she saw the same intensity in the water as she did in her sister's face. Fitting, she thought. An intense ocean for Eliza's wedding day. That seemed about right.

Finally, Eliza turned back to her. She was smiling, bizarrely enough.

"Why on earth are you smiling?" Sara asked, bewildered.

"Because I'm proud of you," Eliza answered simply.

"I'm gonna need you to explain how that relates to anything we're talking about."

Eliza's smile just grew a notch. "A year ago, you wouldn't have hesitated to pull the trigger."

Sara started to say something, then stopped. Eliza was right. The old Sara would've gone sprinting to a newspaper as soon as Benny's email hit her inbox. Her first and only thought would have been to destroy the person who hurt her. Anger—rash, unthinking, immediate—was her default reaction.

Not so much anymore, it seemed.

"Yeah," Sara said softly. She looked down to where Eliza's fingers were intertwined with hers. "Maybe you're right."

"I'm your big sister; of course I'm right."

The women laughed and looked each other in the eye again. Sara was struck for a moment by how much of their father was in Eliza's face. She had that twinkle in her eye, kind of halfway between kindly and all-knowing, like a smart aleck Santa Claus.

"I want to tell you something else, too," Eliza continued. "I see so much of Dad in you."

Sara straightened up at that. The coincidence was freaky. Here she was, thinking about how much her sister looked like their dad, and Eliza said the exact same thing right back to her? "What do you mean?"

"Well, you're stubborn as all get-out. But you're learning how to do it in the right way. You're stubborn where it matters. With your restaurant, with Joey—you went out and got everything you wanted. I admire that. I admire you. You've always been the strongest one in our family, so I'm just ... I'm just happy that you're happy, is what I'm trying to say."

Sara sat still, stunned. This wasn't like them. She and Eliza were fairly close, yes, but not like this. And yet, it felt like something in her heart clicked into place. Like she'd always wanted—no, *needed*—to hear these words from her big sister.

She wished she knew what to say back, but she was scared that, if she opened her mouth, she was going to cry. So she did the only other thing she knew to do—she leaned forward and pulled Eliza into the tightest hug she could manage. They sat there and held each other like that for a while, while the gulls cried outside the window and the sun kept shining through the windows.

A knock on the door interrupted them. Holly and Mom were here. Sara reluctantly released her sister and the two of them straightened up, dabbing tears from the corners of their eyes. Everyone swept into the room, including the hairdressers. Eliza turned the music up and happy chatter filled the air.

Sara ducked into a corner for one moment and fished her cell phone out of her bag. Pulling open a text message, she typed something out and hit send.

Benny: trash the docs. Let it go. Not worth the fight.

She felt lighter at once.

26

MAE

Leanne, the wedding planner, stuck her head in the bridal prep room. She was a smart, competent woman, the kind who looked like she was always carrying a clipboard and wearing a walkie-talkie headset even when she was doing nothing of the sort. That's how Oliver had described her, at least, which made Mae laugh.

"Mae?" Leanne said brightly. "Think I could steal you for a second?"

"Of course!" Mae was in full hummingbird mode, buzzing around happily anywhere she was needed this morning. The ceremony was going to take place on the beach, but they'd rented a small cottage for the day that would house all the preparatory tasks. Later this evening, the reception would take place in the yard, which was a lush green carpet with fairy lights strung across the tree branches that encircled the property. Mae had been there since early in the morning, taking care of everything. She'd gotten Grady and Alice squared away with some activities in one corner, directed Holly to the bridal room, conferred with caterers and Leanne and any number of other people who were involved in all the proceedings. It was a perfect Mae day. Love in the air, lots to do, and a beautiful Nantucket morning to do it all in.

She followed Leanne out of the building, across the yard, and down the walkway that led to the beach, chatting idly about all the different tasks that were underway.

But when they cleared the dunes and she saw the completed setup for the ceremony, it took her breath away. She froze in her tracks, hands clapped over her mouth.

The backdrop was pure Nantucket beauty. Waves lapped delicately at the soft sand, set underneath a sky of cerulean blue that looked like a velvet ceiling stretching far above. Way in the distance, she saw the coiled knot of roiling gray clouds that was the hurricane. She'd thanked her lucky stars again and again that the threat of the storm hadn't come to fruition. She still couldn't quite believe their luck. Truth be told, she suspected Henry had something to do with it. He'd stalled the storm way out to sea to protect his baby girl's big day. If she closed her eyes, she could just picture Happy Henry, tapping his fingertips together merrily, blue eyes twinkling.

But, as gorgeous as the setting was, the decorations themselves were even more fabulous. When Oliver and Eliza had first pitched their general idea for the setup to Leanne, the woman had sat bolt upright in her chair with the faraway look of an artist in her eye. "I know the perfect thing," she'd said. "Do you trust me?" Mae had convinced Eliza to trust the woman, and—well, the proof was in the pudding.

"Leanne, it's—it's—oh my goodness, there aren't even words."

Leanne smiled. "I thought you'd like it."

"Like it" didn't even begin to cover it. Mae felt her heart melt and shape up and melt again.

The white sand stretched in all directions. Leading from the foot of the path they were on towards the water was a walkway festooned on both sides with flowers in every shade of pink and purple. The walkway itself meandered up to the mouth of a massive arch. The flowers climbed unbroken straight from the sand up the sides of the arch, as if they had grown there. They dazzled, studded amongst the green leaves like jewels in a crown. The scent of the flowers carried on the breeze and over to Mae. Beyond the entryway arch, beach and garden flowed together and met at the "altar," which was a perfectly circular wreath nearly ten feet in diameter. It, too, was made of leaves and flowers woven together in soft, delightful hues. It looked like a telescope, like an eye open to the ocean, like a doorway from one life into the next.

Mae turned to Leanne and hugged her, speechless. "You have outdone yourself, lady," she teased.

"Do you think she'll like it?" Leanne asked.

Mae nodded fervently. "She's going to absolutely love it."

The two women stood still for a moment longer, just admiring the spectacle that Leanne had put together. Mae still didn't quite believe that all this was happening.

Then, she felt her phone vibrating in her pocket. "Oh! Excuse me for just a moment, if you don't mind. Someone is calling me." There was no contact assigned to the number. She stepped back towards the cottage a few yards and answered. "Hello?"

"Mrs. Benson?"

"Yes? May I ask who is calling?"

"This is Mrs. Murphy. I'm Father Murphy's wife."

"Oh, of course! How are you, darling?"

Mae heard the woman draw in a short breath and sigh. "I'm afraid I have some extremely unfortunate news. My husband fell down the stairs this morning and broke his leg. We're at the hospital right now getting checked out, and everything seems as though it will be okay, but the long and short of it is that he won't be able to do the ceremony this afternoon."

Mae's jaw dropped. "Oh my goodness gracious."

"I know that's terrible news for you, but—"

"No, no!" Mae interrupted, gnawing at her lip. "My thoughts and prayers are with your husband! We'll be okay. Don't you worry about us. You just tell him to worry about himself. The two of you have always been very good to our family."

She could hear Mrs. Murphy smile and relax. "I'll tell him. Thank you for understanding."

The woman said their goodbyes and hung up. As soon as the call was done, Mae slumped over immediately.

What a horrible break this was! Everything had been shaping up so nicely. But nothing in this world could come off without a hitch, or so it seemed to be with the Benson tribe.

The question now was: what was she supposed to do to fix this?

Striding down the walkway at that moment was Dominic. He was whistling softly, but the wind carried it towards Mae so that it was as if he were standing right next to her. As floored as she was by the news about Father Murphy, she couldn't help but take a moment to admire how dapper Dominic looked in his suit. It was a dark gray number, under which he wore a crisp white shirt and a pale purple tie that matched Mae's dress perfectly. He'd even put on real shoes for the occasion, though Mae had caught him looking longingly at his house slippers when they were getting ready to leave the house that morning.

She was still a bit upset with him. The two of them would have a great deal of very serious talking to do once all the hectic events of this weekend had vanished in the rear-view mirror. The thought of more secrets hiding in the corners of his past life didn't sit well with her. She wanted him to be open with her; it was the only way for their relationship to survive. But their silent reconciliation last night had softened her heart a degree or two.

Perhaps Saoirse was right. Maybe Dominic was truly the saddest man alive. But Mae couldn't help but think that, when they were together, she helped take some small sliver of that sadness away from him. That thought made her happy, because he did the same thing for her. He made her feel like moving forward was possible. All she had to do was reach out and take hold of her future.

Dominic smiled as he neared her, hands in pockets. It wasn't until he got a few steps away that he saw the crestfallen expression on her face and realized that something had gone amiss.

"What is troubling you, my dear?" he asked.

"We don't have a priest," she blurted at once, then quickly explained what had happened.

Dominic's eyes widened. "That is unwelcome news indeed."

Then he fell silent, but in a weird way, like he was searching himself for something. His gaze shifted towards his feet. For some reason, Mae felt a little bit cross at that.

"There isn't a priest hiding under the sand, darling," she snapped.

Dominic raised his gaze back up to hers and cleared his throat. "I ... I may have a solution."

There was that faraway look in his face again. Did he truly have more secrets already? What could possibly be so intimidating that he couldn't say it right away?

"Well? I'm all ears, love." Her words were nice, but she didn't feel very nice at all.

He cleared his throat again, clasped his hands behind his back, shuffled his shoes nervously on the slats of the boardwalk.

"Dominic."

He sighed. "Saoirse is licensed."

"Licensed? What does that even—oh." Realization hit Mae like a pile of bricks. "You don't mean ... oh no."

She hadn't meant to say the last part out loud, but it had slipped between her lips before she could catch it.

Their talk on the beach had gone a long way towards dissipating some of the enmity that hung between the two women. But the truth of the matter was that Saoirse was largely an unwelcome presence in Mae's world. Before her arrival, life had been simple and sweet, easy and good. But she'd come barging in like a boat going too fast in a no-wake zone, stirring up all kinds of muck and nonsense that would've been better off lying undisturbed on the seabed.

Mae understood the reasons now, of course. She saw why Saoirse felt that she had to come.

But that didn't mean that she had to like it.

This was supposed to be a Benson family day. Eliza's day. Hadn't her eldest gone through enough trials? Now, one more unexpected fork in the road. Some might say that it wasn't a big deal. Mae could almost see that phrase bubbling up to Dominic's lips, though it appeared he was wise enough to swallow the words before speaking them out loud to her. But Mae felt otherwise. It *was* a big deal. Eliza deserved a perfect day. She deserved her mother's full attention and love.

Surely, though, that meant letting Saoirse perform the ceremony? The only one who would suffer if Mae put her foot down here was her own daughter.

So, as much as Mae didn't like the thought of seeing her boyfriend's ex-wife reciting the words that would bind Oliver and Eliza together as husband and wife—well, it didn't seem like she had much of a choice.

She exhaled, trying to quell her irritation. Then she glanced up at Dominic and nodded once, tightly. He nodded back and pivoted around to go back and tell Saoirse to get ready for the spotlight.

Mae stood on the boardwalk for a couple of long minutes until Leanne came up behind her. She touched her gently on the elbow. "Are you all right, Mrs. Benson?"

Taking one more long, slow breath, Mae opened her eyes and looked at her. The circular wreath behind the altar framed Leanne's head like a flowery halo. It looked beautiful, as did the sky and the ocean beyond.

Let it go, Mae told herself. She forced a smile across her face and laid her hand on top of Leanne's.

"Everything will be fine, dear," she said. "It always is."

27

ELIZA

Eliza had never been so nervous in her entire life.

She knew full well that it was stupid to be nervous. This was a small gathering of friends and family. Everyone in attendance knew her well. They all loved her. They'd tickled her daughter and shaken hands with her soon-to-be husband and broken bread at their house at one point or another.

But, as she stood at the entrance to the walkway that would separate her old life from the married life she was about to begin, she felt like she might melt into a puddle of anxiety. She glanced over at Leanne, who was standing at her side with a broad, encouraging smile on her face, radio in hand, ready to tell her team stationed down at the beach that the bride was about to enter.

"Ready?" she said, raising the walkie-talkie to her mouth, thumb on the trigger.

"Wait."

Leanne's hand fell by her side. A concerned look came across her face. "Is something wrong, hon?"

"I can't do this."

By "this," she meant walk down the aisle by herself. Since the moment Oliver had first proposed to her at the airport in New York, she had pictured this exact set of events. It made her break out in a cold sweat every time. Her hands would shake, and she'd have to clamp them together or sit on them.

Eliza had taken her father's loss perhaps the best of any of the family —or, more accurately, the least visibly. She knew, deep down, that she was aching in her own way. But Eliza's pain was a private affair. She didn't invite others to the spectacle, the way Brent and Sara did. She needed to lick her wounds in the darkness, alone. And she'd done that in spades, but maybe she wasn't quite as healed up as she thought she was. Because, as she stood here with the Nantucket sun just past overhead, she'd never felt colder or lonelier. Her father was supposed to be here with her. She was supposed to feel his reassuring touch on her elbow, his strength at her side, telling her that everything was going to be okay.

Instead, she felt hollow. Isolated. She could've sworn the temperature in the air dropped or the sun passed behind a cloud or something, because there were goose bumps radiating down her spine.

She looked at herself. The dress was a soft, creamy silk, with thin straps over her shoulders, flowing down into gentle folds past her ankles. The makeup artist and hairdresser had each done beautiful work. When she'd looked in the mirror in the bridal room and taken a big, deep breath, she felt pretty, she felt happy, she felt ready.

All that strength had vanished now. Like water sucked down the drain, no trace of it was left.

It wasn't right that her father was gone. It wasn't fair. And, though she hadn't known it, she wasn't yet finished grieving him.

She felt a tear roll down her cheek. Leanne stepped forward. "Oh, honey," she said in a soft, sweet voice. She touched Eliza's shoulder gently. "Do you want me to call someone back here?"

Eliza thought about it. Ever since she began picturing her walk down the aisle, she'd pictured doing it alone. She wanted her father by her side, of course, but if she couldn't have him, then she wouldn't have anyone. She was a strong, independent woman. She could show her friends, her family, her world that it was okay to be alone sometimes. Hadn't her whole life been about that? It was lonely at the top of the mountain, but that was where she'd always wanted to be.

Until she didn't.

Oliver made her feel like it was okay not to seek out the next peak. It was okay to want love. She'd been scared of that for so long. She didn't want to be weak. But she needed love more than she'd ever realized.

So maybe she wasn't ready to do this walk alone. Maybe she never would be. In this moment, though, that didn't seem like such a weakness.

Because the truth was that she had loved ones who would walk with her. She didn't have to fight against sorrow and grief as an army of one. She could call for support.

Eliza looked up at Leanne. "I want my mom," she whispered.

Eliza could hear the shuffle and murmurs of the crowd. There were forty-five people in attendance—small, intimate, just the way she wanted things. But right now, they were all hidden behind the curve in the path. It was just her and her mother. They had maybe half a dozen steps before they broke out into the open and everybody saw them.

But before they did that, Eliza wanted to look her mother in the face once more. She stopped and glanced over. "You look beautiful, Mom," she said.

Mom smiled in that Mom way she had, the way no one else except maybe Dad knew how to smile. It was a smile that said, "The world is perfect right now because you are my daughter and I am your parent and nothing—not a single gosh-darn thing—can ever, ever change that." Mom didn't have to say those words out loud. Her smile did it for her.

"*You* are the beauty today, my darling." Mom rested one palm lightly on Eliza's neck.

Eliza closed her eyes and savored the moment for as long as she could. She felt the wrinkles on her mother's fingertips. She felt the warmth of her body, the pulse of her heartbeat. The breeze stirred the long grasses around them, casting a soft shushing sound like bedsheets rustling.

"I love you," she said when she opened her eyes.

"I love you, too," Mom said. "Now let's go get you married."

Laughing, the two of them took the last of the steps that remained. Mom squeezed her elbow as they made their way under the first arch.

The crowd gasped as one. Eliza couldn't help but smile. She didn't feel like she had to cry anymore. She felt like laughing actually, like joy was flowing through her bloodstream and filling her so there was no room for anything else but that.

Oliver was standing in front of the flower halo. It was jaw-droppingly gorgeous. He was wearing a navy tuxedo, close to black, but just shy of it, so that the blue of the ocean, the blue of the bluebonnets, and the blue of his outfit all flowed together magnificently. He was smiling, but she could swear she saw the glimmer of a tear in one corner of his eye. She couldn't wait to tease him about that later. They had a running bet about which of them would cry first. Loser got cake in the face at the reception. Eliza didn't much mind whether she won or lost.

At the end of the aisle, they stopped. Eliza leaned over and gave her mother a kiss on the cheek. Then she straightened up and admired her for one more second. Mom was so strong. She'd been through more than anyone should have to go through, and yet somehow she still had the strength to lend to Eliza when she needed it most. She looked beautiful today, too, with her hair in loose curls and sapphire earrings matching her necklace. She was nearing her mid-sixties, yes, but her vitality glistened despite the crows' feet at the corner of her eyes and the subtle graying of her hair. She looked more alive than Eliza could ever remember.

Then it was time to go meet her fiancé at the altar. She and Mom parted ways. Oliver smiled again as Eliza mounted the low platform and took her place across from him. Dominic's ex-wife Saoirse stood between them. Mom had explained something to Eliza about the minister falling, but she made Eliza promise not to worry about it. Saoirse seemed nice enough, if strangely mysterious. But it seemed right somehow, weirdly enough. There was almost a little bit of magic in the woman's eyes, like she knew something about the ways of the world that not many other people did. Eliza wasn't sure whether to chalk it up to pure eccentricity, to her Irish heritage, or something else altogether. Well, those were questions for another time. For now, she turned her gaze to Oliver.

She let herself take in all the details of his face. She wanted to memorize this moment so she could close her eyes and picture it anytime she chose for the rest of her life.

There was a faint scar that ran from his right eyebrow up to his forehead before disappearing in his thicket of hair. His nose was strong and proud, a sharp line straight as an arrow. Those lips—soft, strong, perpetually twitching with a wry smile—were somehow both gentle and solemn right now. As always, she saved his eyes for last. Those were the first things she had ever noticed about him, that night he'd spilled a beer on her in that Nantucket bar. They were brimming with life, green and playful. An artist's eyes.

He reached out and took her hands in his. After his eyes, his hands were her favorite feature of Oliver's. They were lithe and strong. She loved watching his fingers stroke the keys of a piano whenever he let her sit and watch him play. Like his eyes, his hands had more life in them than others' did. The music was in his hands, he always said. He was just the one who was chosen to carry them around. That always made her laugh. Funny and serious and ethereal all at once—that was her Oliver. That was her love.

Saoirse cleared her throat and began reciting the words, but Eliza didn't or couldn't or chose not to hear them. They didn't matter much. This wasn't about saying one thing or another. Oliver and Eliza had already said everything that needed to be said. They'd made the choices, again and again, every day for lots of days running now, to be with each other and to be a family to her little girl. So she kept staring into his eyes and running her thumb over the backs of his knuckles while Saoirse's lilting Irish accent rose up and down, almost in time with the waves. Seagulls squawked overhead every now and then. Eliza imagined that they were shouting "Hear hear!" and "Amen!" at particularly stirring parts of Saoirse's speech.

Eliza turned to look at the crowd. They were all seated in white folding chairs aligned in neat rows. She saw Oliver's adopted parents, Neal and Marcy. She saw Brent and Rose, with Susanna between them, swinging her legs because they weren't long enough to reach the ground. She saw Mom, Sara, Joey, Holly, Pete, Alice, Grady. She saw Sheriff Mike, looking hilariously uncomfortable in a suit. She saw Debra and a handsome older man. A new beau, perhaps? Mom had mentioned something about her trying online dating now. Maybe it had been successful.

Then, before she could finish looking around and taking stock of who was here, it was time for her and Oliver to exchange vows.

Saoirse looked to Eliza. "Repeat after me, love. I, Eliza Benson ..."

"I, Eliza Benson ..."

"... take thee, Oliver Patterson ..."

"... take thee, Oliver Patterson ..."

"... to be my wedded husband, to have and to hold, from this day forward ..."

"... to be my wedded husband, to have and to hold, from this day forward ..."

"... for better, for worse, in sickness and in health, to love and to cherish ..."

"... for better, for worse, in sickness and in health, to love and to cherish ..."

"... till death do us part."

"... till death do us part."

Eliza squeezed Oliver's hands. A life with him. It was here. It was beginning. It was now.

She couldn't wait to get started.

28

SARA

Saturday night.

"Time to drink!" Joey crowed as they walked up to the yard behind the cottage where the reception was taking place.

"Shush!" Sara admonished, pinching him in the side.

"Ow! What'd I say?"

"It's time to *celebrate love,*" she corrected with a wicked grin.

Joey growled and pounced on her before she knew what was happening. He grabbed her by the waist with one hand and put his other hand in the middle of her back as he swooped her into a low dip and kissed her fiercely. By the time he stood her up, her head was spinning.

"Whoa," she muttered, trying to regain her balance.

"There we go," Joey said triumphantly. His grin matched Sara's now. "Love has been celebrated. *Now* it's time to drink."

Sara laughed, rolled her eyes, and grabbed Joey's hand. Together, they walked into the party.

It was a gorgeous scene. The fairy lights that had been strung amongst the tree branches cast a warm glow over all the partiers, like a ceiling of light. An open bar in one corner of the yard glistened with bottles of wine, beer, and liquor. Along the left-hand side, long linen-covered tables groaned under the weight of silver plates and cutlery, eagerly awaiting dinner. Waiters were circulating with hors oeuvres— pimento cheese and prosciutto biscuits, red potatoes with tomato-avocado salsa, little red lentil terrines and bruschetta. Sara couldn't help but burst out laughing when she glanced over at her boyfriend and saw that his mouth was already stuffed full. Joey didn't hesitate to sample each of the snacks on offer.

They went and found the family to say their hellos. Mom was chatting away with Debra and her new man. He was outrageously tall, over six and a half feet, but he had a nice muscular build to go with it and a handsome head of thick salt-and-pepper hair. He and Debra looked smitten with each other, if their flitting glances back and forth and mysterious smiles were anything to go by.

Eliza was constantly occupied, of course, talking to everyone at once, so Sara just snuck in and gave her sister a quick kiss on the cheek and a promise to connect later in the evening.

Holly was busy trying to convince Grady to try a prawn. Sara wisely chose to steer clear of that.

The first part of the evening rolled by in a blur. Sara held Joey's hand tightly as the attendees cleared the center of the yard for Eliza and Oliver to share their first dance. Oohs and ahhs filtered out of the crowd as the lovebirds held each other close and spun in a slow, easy circle to the sounds of a beautiful country song Sara didn't recognize. She thought Oliver had a funny expression on his face at the very end of the dance after Eliza said something in his ear, but maybe she was just imagining things. It was a cute moment either way.

Once the song faded away, the DJ invited the rest of the crowd to join the couple on the dance floor. That was Sara's cue to go turn away and find some snacks of her own.

But to her surprise, Joey didn't let go of her hand. He pulled her back into him. "You aren't trying to duck me, are you?"

Sara saw what he was getting at and immediately shook her head firmly. "If you think you're getting me on that dance floor, you must've sustained a head injury or something."

"I thought we were here to celebrate love?"

"Exactly, and I love food, so I'm gonna go celebrate with that crab dip, if I can find the right server."

"You aren't getting away that easily, Chef Sara."

She laughed and tried to pull away, but he still wasn't letting go. "Joey Burton," she warned.

His grin split his face in two. "I do love when you say my name like that ..."

"I'm serious," she said again, eyebrows raised as threateningly as she could make them. "Unhand me at once."

"Is this your serious boss voice?" he teased. "I kinda like it."

Slowly but surely, he was tugging her towards the dance floor, which had begun to fill up with other couples twirling each other about. This was Sara's nightmare, her Kryptonite. For all her bravado, she had never, ever been a dancer. And she didn't plan on starting tonight.

But her boyfriend—her infuriatingly cute, relentless boyfriend—had other ideas.

"Just one song," he said.

"Nope."

"Half a song."

"Nuh-uh."

"A chorus. One measly chorus."

"Joey ..."

The song shifted into the next and his eyes lit up. "Oh yes, this one is perfect. C'mon."

"You really aren't going to take no for an answer, are you?"

He softened, his face falling into a hangdog expression. "Okay, fine. I guess you're just embarrassed that I'll out-dance you."

Sara snorted. "I'm already mentally prepared to have bruises on the top of my feet."

"You're just scared. I get it. I understand."

She wrinkled her brow skeptically. "I see what you're doing, you know."

He spread his arms wide. "Who, me? I'm just making sure my girlfriend doesn't get all terrified, you know? It's a big, scary place, the dance floor at a wedding, and if you're not careful ..."

Sara was rolling her eyes as hard as she possibly could, but she sighed, growled, and tugged Joey onto the dance floor all at once. He cackled like a loon as he pulled her close to him and they began to dance. "That was easy."

"You'll pay for this, Burton."

He closed his eyes and smacked his lips like he was savoring something delicious. "The boss voice strikes again. Make me pay, chef."

She didn't even have the heart to shush him again. He was like a puppy dog—brimming with boundless, irresistibly contagious energy. It was impossible for her to look at him and not smile.

Especially tonight, with how handsome he looked in his formal attire. The lines of his shoulders were broad and strong, and as they swayed and spun together to the music, she was surprised by how capably he was leading her. For a change, she let herself be led. It was nice. She spent all her days and nights being the boss at Little Bull. It was in her nature to want to be in charge. But here, tonight, it was an unexpected relief to close her eyes and let the music and her boyfriend guide her. Nothing to worry about, nothing to dictate, nothing to choose. She felt light on her feet, practically weightless. The night was beautiful, her sister was married, and she was being swept away in the arms of a man who understood implicitly how her brain and heart operated.

It was okay to let go here.

She fell silent and laid her head against his chest. Joey's heart beat almost in time to the music as it slowed into a quiet fade-out.

She wasn't sure how long they remained there before she heard another man clear his throat to her left. Glancing up in surprise, she saw Russell Bridges standing there with a smile on his face. He looked to Joey. "Mind if I cut in for a moment?" he asked.

Joey glanced down at Sara. "If it's all right with the lady."

Sara looked back and forth between the men, then broke out into a soft smile of her own. "It's okay, J," she said. She stood up on her tiptoes—Joey was far taller than her, even when she was wearing high heels—and kissed him on the lips. "Go find us some good snacks. I'll be over in a minute."

He nodded, then left her and Russell facing each other on the dance floor. Bodies flowed around them before he offered his hand to her. She took it delicately and the two of them joined the current as the next song picked up tempo.

"Wasn't sure if you were going to come," Sara commented, eyeing Russell.

"And miss this? You're crazy. It's open bar, you know."

Sara laughed and punched him in the chest. He was as solid as ever. Might've even been working out, if the thickness of his muscle was anything to go by. "Where's Clarissa?"

"Off flirting with other men, no doubt."

"Oh?"

He grinned. "I'm just kidding. She's snacking at our table. I told her I just wanted to steal a quick dance from my favorite Benson lady."

"Now I'm your favorite Benson?"

"No, but you're the only one I could find." He grinned again as she punched him for the second time.

"You haven't changed a bit, you know," she told him.

"Is that such a bad thing?"

"No," she decided. "I don't think it is."

"Let's hope so. I'm more than halfway through my thirties. The window for change is closing quickly."

"Don't put it like that; you're depressing me."

"You and me both."

They moved and spun slowly, like the second hand of a clock sweeping around its face. "How're you guys?" Sara asked, meaning Russell and Clarissa.

"We're great," he said at once. His eyes sort of clouded over in that lovey-dovey way that she'd seen in Joey from time to time when he didn't think she was looking at him. She loved that expression in her man. It was actually cute to see it in Russell, too. "I'm thinking ..." He looked around suspiciously, as if to make sure no one was looking. "I'm thinking of popping the question next year."

Sara yelped, then bit her lip to catch it before Clarissa noticed, wherever she was. She couldn't help but smile, though. "No way! Russ, that's amazing. I'm so happy for you guys."

"So you better save the date." He winked. "And schedule your dance with me right now, because I'll be a hot, hot commodity that night."

"You're always a hot commodity, Bridges."

"You know me too well, Miss Benson."

He looked handsome in the fairy lights, and practically oozing with happiness. It was heartwarming to see him this way. Once upon a time, it would have made her heart eat itself in anger. Anger that it wasn't her he was loving, anger that someone could move on and leave her behind. Now, though, she could honestly look at him and feel nothing but joy on his behalf.

Eliza was right. She was growing up.

Their dance brought them around to one of the high-top tables and Sara saw Clarissa standing there. She waved her over. The little blonde thing came bouncing up, all smiles, and Sara stepped back. "Your man won't shut up about you," she said to her with a wry grin.

Clarissa laughed. "One of his best and worst qualities. You learn to live with it, ya know?"

"Believe me, I know. You two go canoodle. I'm gonna go hunt down my dinner."

She waved and left Clarissa and Russell to the crush of the dance floor while she went to find Joey. She didn't see him on her first half-circle of the party, but she realized she was near her spot at the table where she'd left her purse hanging on the back of her chair, so she stopped to get some ChapStick out.

As she dug in the contents of her bag, she felt the rustle of paper on her fingertips. She paused. She could feel her heartbeat thudding in her throat all of a sudden. *Ba-boom. Ba-boom.* Slowly, she withdrew it and opened it up. It was well-worn, creased, thumbed over a thousand times.

The Martin Hogan review.

The title leapt off the page at her, just like it always did. *Arrogance Meets Incompetence in New Nantucket Wannabe* ... But for some reason, it didn't have the same sting tonight as it had every other night since the day it was published. Normally, she could count on feeling her stomach churn and her heart drop as soon as she opened the sheet up.

Not now. Now tonight.

She felt Joey walk up behind her before she saw him. His chin, sandpaper-rough from shaving for the event, nestled against her neck and his hands encircled her waist. "Whatcha got there?" he asked. But as soon as he saw it, she could feel him darken. "We talked about that, Sara."

She turned to face him. "I know." She saw the concern written on his face. He was an empathetic creature. She knew that his heart hurt on her behalf each and every time she tortured herself with the words of this petty, vicious man and the petty, vicious man who'd compelled him to write them. Gavin, Martin—they were goblins. Nothing more.

So she decided—suddenly and irrevocably—that she didn't have room in her life for them anymore.

She needed that room for other things. For love, for Joey, for her restaurant, for her family, for her friends. For looking up at the beautiful star-studded Nantucket night sky, where it glimmered beyond the reach of the fairy lights, and for realizing that she was blessed beyond all measure to live here.

"Come with me." She grabbed his hand. He hesitated for a moment, unsure what she wanted. "Come on! I want you with me for this."

Sara led Joey to the walkway that led to the beach. Together, they went down the planks, leaving the hubbub and lights of the reception behind them. There was a small bonfire and some chairs out here for people to duck away from the party to catch a breath of fresh air. The sound of the waves surrounded them and wrapped them up like a quilt.

The sand was soft under Sara's feet as she slipped off her high heels and hitched up her dress with one hand so it didn't drag amongst the dunes. She and Joey approached the fire. It emanated heat in crackling waves.

By the light of the fire, she glanced at the review one last time. These words were poison, and she'd been willingly drinking it night after night for months now. So why keep doing it? Why not do the one thing she'd been unwilling to do for her whole entire life?

Why not just ... let go?

One by one, her fingers loosened, until the crinkled sheet, worn smooth by her touch, was held between just her thumb and forefinger.

Then she let that go, too.

It caught the wind, flipped once, and landed in the middle of the fire. The flames licked away at the edges. It didn't take long before the whole thing was engulfed in fire and turning to black. She saw Martin Hogan's name last of all.

Then it was gone.

All of it. Her spite, her jealousies, her self-doubt. Old Sara burned up in the flames.

New Sara turned to Joey, who hadn't let go of her hand. She kissed him, soft at first, then hard, grabbing the back of his neck and pulling him to her. His smell filled her nose and his hands found her hips and the fire and the ocean swelled around them and it was a moment too full of all things beautiful to leave room for anything as ugly and twisted as the things she once insisted on keeping with her.

She kissed her boyfriend until her calves ached from standing on her tiptoes. But no sooner had she separated and returned to earth than Joey's belly rumbled.

He grinned sheepishly, for fear he had ruined an important moment. But Sara laughed. This, too, was perfect.

"Told you I'm always hungry."

"That you did," she said. "Let's go get some food."

29

BRENT

Brent was on a mission.

It had been a long time since he'd felt this way. Since when? Before Dad, maybe. His vision had narrowed down to a tunnel. Nothing else could distract him. It was a strange way to be feeling on the night of his sister's wedding, yeah, but he wasn't going to be stopped.

He needed to find Rose's daughter.

She'd done a fabulous job as flower girl at the ceremony that afternoon. The crowd loved her on sight as she skipped down the aisle casting rose petals left and right. With braided blonde buns and a frilly little dress, she was a poster child for what a flower girl was supposed to look like. Brent had worn a massive, cheesy smile the whole time.

That was only one of the many little moments he'd had all day long of falling further in love with his life. He felt—so strongly, so powerfully, so tangibly—his blessings surrounding him. Family. Friends. Love, love, love. Surely there was no one else in the world this lucky. How could there be? He had it all.

There she was. He saw a flash of blonde hair streak past a dozen yards ahead of him. She was headed towards the quiet area with the fire out on the beach. He tried calling after her, but she must not have heard him, because she just kept running. Grimacing, he set off the way she'd gone.

It was a clear night, though he could still see the hurricane boiling at the very edge of the horizon, a spot a little darker than the rest of the night sky. He felt the warm twin buzz of happiness and champagne in his bloodstream.

But he needed to focus. He had a mission to accomplish.

"Susanna!" he called again. He saw her little shape turn around by the fire as he walked up into the circle of light. "There you are."

She grinned and waved at him. "That's a big fire!" she said, pointing at the flames.

"Yes, it sure is," he agreed.

"Can we make s'mores?"

"Maybe after. Hey, Suz, can I ask you something?" He knelt to her level.

She put her hands behind her back in that shy little girl way as soon as he got down to her level. It made him laugh every time she did that. No matter how close they grew, he would always be Mr. B to her. Well, maybe not always. Not if this mission was a success.

"Can I?"

"Yeah," she replied in a tiny voice.

"Do you promise to keep it a secret for just a little while?"

"Okay."

He fished in his pocket and pulled out a small velvet box. "I got your mommy a gift," he whispered. Cracking the box open, he showed

Susanna the engagement ring that sat on a plush cushion within. "Do you think it's pretty?"

Her eyes widened. She nodded, looking back and forth between his face and the ring. "Yeah!"

"Good. I think so, too. I'm glad you agree."

"Are you going to give that to Mommy?"

Brent shifted his weight and retrieved something else from his pocket, though he hid that in his palm for a moment longer. "Well, maybe. But I had to find you so I could ask you something first."

"What do you have to ask me?" she mumbled, curious.

"You see, if I give your mom this ring, that means I'm asking her to marry me."

"Like Aunt 'Liza got married today?"

"Exactly. Do you know what that means?"

She nodded.

"Can you tell me?"

"It means being in love forever and ever and ever and ever."

Brent laughed. "Bingo. So if I give your mom this ring, it means I want to be in love with her forever and ever and ever and ever."

"Okay," she said again.

He continued, "But before I can do that, I have to ask *you* first." He cracked open the second box and showed the inside to her. It was a smaller version of the first ring (sans-diamond, of course), sized for a child's finger. "I want to love your mom forever. But I want to love you forever, too. So I got you a ring. And I want to get your permission before I give your mommy's ring to her. If you say yes, then we can be a happy family. You don't have to say yes if you don't want to, though."

She grabbed his hand and squealed, "Yes, yes, yes!"

Brent was fighting to hold back a tear that he never saw coming. Luckily, the shadows of the night hid it from anyone who might be watching across the fire. "Well, hold out your hand then." Susanna held out her hand for him and he slipped the small ring onto her finger. It was a little big, but it would do for now. They could put it on a necklace when she outgrew it, perhaps.

"Can I have a hug?" he asked. Susanna threw herself at him, nearly knocking him onto his back in the sand. He *oofed*, laughed, squeezed her tight.

She was six years old, probably too young to fully grasp all the implications of what he was asking her. But she knew enough that he valued her saying yes. And when he hugged her, he tried to tell her all the things with his hug that she maybe didn't quite understand in his words. That he would love her. That he would protect her. That he would be a father to her, for as long as she would have him.

That moment meant far more to him than he had realized until the very second it was happening.

Eventually, he let her go and set her down. "Can I ask you one more favor?" he said.

She nodded again. One blonde braid had begun to unravel. He reached up and smoothed it behind her ear with a gentle hand.

"Can you go get your mommy for me? But Suz—" He grabbed her before she could run off. "Make sure you don't give away our secret just yet, okay?"

She nodded, giggled, then took off running back towards the party, her bare feet kicking up plumes of sand as she went.

Brent sank back onto his heels and dabbed his tear away with the cuff of his shirt. Closing his eyes, he took a deep breath. Salty air mixed with the woodsy smoke from the fire. He listened to the crackling logs and the slap of waves on the shore, and as he did, he offered up a quiet thanks to his father, wherever he might be.

He opened his eyes when he heard someone approaching. The light picked up Rose a few yards away. He smiled and took to his feet as she approached. "You look incredible," he whispered, half to her and half to himself. He wasn't lying. In a wine-colored dress that swung past her ankles, with her hair piled artfully on top of her head, she was the belle of the ball. She'd taken off her heels, he saw, and had them clasped together in one hand as she walked up to him and offered her lips up for a gentle kiss.

"You're not so bad yourself," she hummed back. "Now, what's all the fuss about? Susanna made it seem like there was a house on fire."

"Let's take a walk," Brent said instead of answering. Threading his fingers through hers, they went strolling down the beach, away from the light of the fire. The moon was bright tonight. It lit up the sand and the water until the whole scene almost glowed. He could sense Rose's curiosity, but he smiled to himself. *Let her be curious for a little longer,* he thought. *There'll be time for answers soon.*

"Do you think Henrietta is okay?" she asked when they'd gone thirty or forty slow strides down away from the party.

They'd left her with a neighbor to watch over for the night. She was due to give birth to her litter any day now. Brent laughed to himself. Both he and his dog were about to become parents, in a roundabout sort of way. Life had a funny way of moving in lockstep with itself.

"She's going to be a great mom," he said.

He felt Rose look at him and chuckle. "That wasn't really the question," she teased. "Where's your head at, space cadet?"

Brent stopped and turned to face her. He put his hands on her hips and pulled her close to him. "It's right here," he answered with the utmost seriousness. "Right in this moment, with you."

Rose's smile disappeared, replaced with something more somber and searching. Her eyes raked over his face, looking for some explanation as to his unusual mood. "That's awfully romantic for a handyman," she said quietly.

"Blame it on the champagne."

"Ah. Liquid courage."

"No," he corrected with a shake of his head. "I've wanted to say this to you for a long time."

She tilted her head to the side to fix him with a curious gaze. "All right," she said. "Enough crypticness. Say what?"

In response, Brent stepped back and dropped to one knee. Rose froze at once. It felt like the world began to unroll slowly, so slowly, slowly enough that he had time to notice all the details of this moment. He was glad for that, because it meant that he could save them away and look back at them over and over whenever he wanted, like photos of your loved ones stored in your wallet.

Rose's face was heavy in the shadow, but her eyes were bright, and that was all he needed to see.

"Rose," he began, "I've loved you since before I knew that I did. Since that first day on the beach. Before I knew your name or your story, I loved you. I was a mess back then, and to say you saved me doesn't even begin to do it justice. You are my rock, my light, my love. And I want to spend the rest of my life loving you."

He noticed a tear sliding down her face only when it caught the moonlight and refracted it into a million little moonbeams, like a crystal clinging to the edge of her lip.

"I hope you're not too mad, though, because you're actually the second person I gave a ring to tonight. Susanna liked hers, so I hope you like yours just as much. Make me two for two, Rose. Tell me you'll marry me."

Rose laughed—the most beautiful sound he knew—and she fell to her knees across from him. Placing a hand on either side of her face, she pulled him into a tearstained kiss. "Yes," she whispered when she broke the kiss off. "Yes, you crazy man. Yes, I'll marry you."

They went through the delicate, trembling ritual of sliding the ring onto her finger. She kissed him again.

Then Brent got a crazy gleam in his eye.

Rose noticed and asked, "What else could you possibly have cooked up?"

He grinned wildly. "What about now?"

"What on earth are you talking about?"

"Marry me right now."

"What? How?"

"Will you?"

"I mean, yes—what? I'm lost, babe."

Brent clambered to his feet. "Stay right there," he commanded. "Don't move a muscle. I'll be right back."

He ran as fast as he could back up the beach, back down the walkway, back into the party. He heard Marshall calling him over to do shots with him and Dr. Dawson, but that would have to wait until later. He came to a halt and looked around the party.

Then he saw what he was looking for.

"Over here!" Brent called back over his shoulder. He saw the dark figure of Rose, outlined where he'd left her on the beach. The thump of footsteps behind him was a few dozen yards back. He came up to

Rose and took her hands, then looked back to where he'd come from to see the person he went to fetch striding up.

Saoirse looked unruffled, which was kind of amazing, given the franticness with which Brent had snatched her away from the party. She'd been quietly drinking a whiskey soda in one corner. If she understood even half of what he'd babbled, that would've been a miracle in and of itself. But she must've gotten the gist of it, because here she was.

"Marry me now," he said again.

Rose looked back and forth between Brent and Saoirse until she finally understood. "You're serious," she laughed.

"I've never been more serious about anything in my life. I don't want to spend another night not married to you."

Rose laughed a second time, but it faded away quickly into a glistening-eyed smile, barely there but all the more beautiful for its subtlety. "Okay," she whispered. "Let's do it."

Brent nodded to Saoirse, who had an enigmatic smile of her own. And then they exchanged vows, there on the beach of Nantucket, with not a soul in the world but the three of them—plus Susanna, who insisted on saying "I do" after her mom—there to witness.

When it was over, Brent kissed Rose. Like he'd done with Susanna, he tried to tell her with his touch everything that he didn't know how to say with his words. That she meant everything to him, that she had saved him. She knew all those things already. But Brent knew that it was nice to be reminded sometimes.

Saoirse bowed and left the way she had come. She was a mysterious force, that one. He'd have to ask Mom or Dominic about her later.

For now, though, he just wanted to sit on the beach and watch the waves with his bride and their little girl.

The night stretched on for a while longer. Brent and Rose decided not to tell anybody what had happened just yet. There was no need to steal Eliza and Oliver's spotlight. Let them have their special night; they more than deserved it.

The two of them went and found Susanna and swept her up into a family hug and left it at that.

Soon, though, it was time to put the little girl to bed. That meant that Brent and Rose needed to be going. He went and found Mom, who was seated with Dominic at their table, watching the dancers in front of the DJ booth. She had a pleasant smile on. Brent suspected she'd had one or two more glasses of wine than she normally allowed herself to drink.

"We gotta get the rascal to bed," Brent told her, jutting his head towards Susanna, who was fast asleep in her mother's arms, braids akimbo.

"Oh, of course, of course!" Mom cried, getting up from her seat. She gave Susanna a kiss on the head and Rose on the cheek.

Watching his mother kiss his wife and daughter filled Brent with a sudden and powerful desire to tell her. He wanted his mom to know that everything was going to be okay. She would worry about him forever, of course—that was a parent's obligation. But maybe, if he let her in on this special secret on this magical night, she'd worry just a little bit less.

"I'll meet you at the car, babe," he told her. "Just wanna talk to my mom real quick about something first." He winked at Rose and she smiled back.

"Okay, hon," she said. "See you in a sec."

Mom had her head tilted quizzically to one side as he turned back to her. "What's all the fuss for?"

"C'mere," he told her, leading her off to a quiet corner of the party. He stopped when he was satisfied that they had a reasonable cone of silence around them. Then he told her what had just happened on the beach.

Mom beamed at once and threw her arms around him. "Oh, honey, I'm so happy for you," she murmured in his ear. "Stay right there."

"Huh?"

"Right there," she repeated, pointing at the spot on the ground where he was standing. "Don't move."

Brent laughed. Oh, how the tables had turned. First, he was the one surprising Rose. Now, his mom had something of her own up her sleeve. There was never any one-upping Momma, he supposed. She was sly like that.

He watched as she went back over to Dominic, who retrieved her purse from the chair he was sitting in. She got something out of it and came back over to him. It was his turn to wait for this big mystery to be revealed.

But when she pressed a key into his hand, he still didn't understand. He held it up to the light. It looked like an ordinary house key.

"What's this?" he asked with a wrinkled brow.

"A wedding present for you," she commented with a foxy smile. "Something you wanted, I think. You can tell your realtor we'll handle the transaction ourselves."

It clicked all of a sudden in his head. When it did, his jaw dropped and he nearly keeled over.

It was the key to the house on Howard Street.

"What did you ... where did you ... I mean, how?!"

Mom smiled wider and squeezed his forearm once. "A mother's intuition," was all she said. Then she turned and went back to

Dominic, leaving Brent standing there with a key in his hand and an utterly bewildered expression on his face.

30

ELIZA

An hour earlier.

The crowd had ebbed backwards towards the outer edge of the cottage garden, leaving a wide swathe of lawn open in the middle. The fairy lights strung overhead caught the dew on the grass, making the whole floor seem shimmery and alive. Eliza heard the DJ croon through his speaker, "Make way, ladies and gentlemen, for the bride and the groom to enjoy their first dance."

She felt hands usher her towards the open expanse. On the opposite side of the circle, she saw Oliver being pushed forward in the same way. They met in the middle as the opening notes of the song they'd chosen filtered out into the night.

It was a soft country duet: "Magnolia Wind," by Emmylou Harris and John Prine. Prine was one of her dad's favorites. He was wry, funny, raspy, soulful. Something about the song made her laugh and cry at the same time. It was so sweetly honest, so innocently vulnerable. And the image of the opening line made her laugh. *I'd rather sleep in a box like a bum on the street / Than a fine feather bed with your little ol' cold feet.* Her mind flashed back to the morning that they'd learned about Clay's crimes. It felt like both forever ago and yesterday all at once. Winter giggling, Oliver teasing, and his cold feet sneaking up her calf. Sweetness. Perfection. All hers, forever, starting right now.

The twin voices of the singers rose, accompanied by the gentle strumming of the guitar. Oliver held Eliza close as they swayed together, rooted in place. Her eyes were closed and her head rested against Oliver's shoulder.

So much had happened to bring her here. A lot of it had hurt. False turns and switchbacks on this road to happiness. But that was the way of the world, she was learning. Just because she'd spent most of her life on a straight climb to the top didn't mean it was always going to be that way. She was learning to be okay with that fact. Call it aging or wisdom or just having the same life lesson beaten into your head enough times until you finally learned it. Whatever it was, it was worth it for the sweetness of this moment right here, right now, in the arms of her husband.

She heard a whimper from the edge of the crowd and a frantic "Wait!" She looked up and saw that Winter had wriggled out of the arms of the babysitter they'd hired to keep an eye on her this evening and come waddling across the empty lawn, crying for her mother.

Oliver looked down smiling as Eliza bent to scoop her daughter up. "Hi, honey," she whispered as she linked back up with Oliver. He held both of them in his embrace and they resumed their swaying as the song began to fall from its final chorus towards the final note like a feather dropping back and forth, back and forth through the warm, humid air. Winter didn't say anything, just buried her face in Eliza's neck and clung to her hair with tight fists.

"My girls," Oliver said quietly. He hadn't stopped smiling all night, not even when Eliza insisted that she had won the bet and smeared a piece of cake right in his face. He'd gotten her back immediately, of course, but that was okay. Everything was okay.

When the song had almost ended, something tugged in Eliza's chest, or rather, plucked at her heartstrings like a chord. This was the moment to tell Oliver the secret she'd held close for a couple of days now. She'd been waiting for the right time to tell him, to make sure everything was perfect. But what could be more perfect than now?

So she leaned up and said, "I have to tell you a secret."

"Uh-oh," he whispered back. "Did someone crash the wedding?"

She grinned. "All the better if they did. We have way too much alcohol, and your cousin is still prowling for a hot date."

"My cousin will be just fine; don't you worry about her," he shot back. "So spill the beans, my beautiful wife. What's your story?"

Eliza laughed, and then she had to bite her lip to stop from crying. *What's your story?* That's what he'd asked her on the night they met. She'd told him the truth then. The whole truth and nothing but the truth. Who she was and where she'd come from and what she wanted and what made her heart hurt. And he'd listened. He'd never stopped listening, not even for a second. Those eyes drank her and her story in and they never gave her back up. That was when she'd started to love him, even if she hadn't known it at the time. She knew now.

"I'm pregnant," she whispered. "We're going to have a baby. You're going to be a father."

Oliver's eyes widened huge and green, as green as the lawn at their feet. Before he could catch himself, another tear started to trickle down his cheek. She laughed, because she was crying, too, and as she reached up and wiped the tear from his face, she added, "I get to pie you again, you know."

"Pie away, my love," he answered without hesitation. "I'm going to be a father." He hugged her and Winter close and kissed each of them on the head. "I love you."

"I love you, too, Oliver. I always will."

Winter went home with the babysitter and Oliver was called away to talk to Neal and Marcy's friends. Eliza found a seat on the edge of the party zone and collapsed gratefully. Her feet were aching something fierce from what had been a very, very long day. A good day, but a long one.

She didn't have long to rest before her mom came up though, holding something in her hands. "You need to eat, love," she chided.

"I know, I know," Eliza said. "In a sec. My legs don't want to work right now."

"Well, I remember how that was," she said with a smile. "Take your time. Here, take this, too." She handed Eliza what she was holding, which turned out to be an old-fashioned parchment envelope, sealed with a red wax stamp. "I hope you won't hold it against me too much if I tell you that this is addressed to both you and your siblings," she added. "I know it's your special day, believe me. But once I started writing, I just couldn't stop."

"Of course not, Mama," Eliza said softly. She glanced down at the envelope and ran her thumb delicately over the seal. "Am I supposed to read it now?"

Mom nodded. "Go find a quiet place, just the four of you, and read it together."

"Okay."

She leaned down and gave Eliza a kiss. "Now, where did I leave my boyfriend?" she mumbled under her breath as she turned and disappeared back into the tide of partygoers.

Eliza closed her eyes and took a few more slow breaths. Then, wincing as she got back to her feet, she went off to find her brother and sisters.

It took her fifteen minutes to wrangle them all. But eventually, they snuck off to the beach and wandered down fifty yards or so from the fire.

"Who's going to read it?" Eliza asked, holding out the letter.

"You are, duh," Sara fired back.

Eliza balked. "Me? Why me?"

"You're the oldest," Holly said. "I thought that was a given."

"I don't want to read it! What if I cry?"

Holly snorted. "As if I won't?"

"Maybe Brent should read it then," Sara suggested.

"Nuh-uh," he said, shaking his head and holding up his hands. "That's not my cup of tea."

"You're the guy."

"And you're the one with a lot of excuses. Maybe *you* should read it."

"Why would I—"

"Shush," Eliza interrupted. "We'll play odds-and-evens. Fair?"

"Fine," everyone grumbled. Odds-and-evens was the age-old Benson method for settling familial arguments. On the count of three, everyone threw up either one or two fingers. Whoever was the odd one out lost. Most times, it was an even split, so they had to keep going until there was only one loser.

But tonight, on the count of three, Eliza looked down and saw that she was the only one holding up two fingers. She groaned. "That's not fair! It's my wedding day!"

"You lost, fair and square," Brent reminded her. "These rules are sacred. No going back."

She wanted to keep complaining, but he was right. Besides, she was the eldest. If anyone was going to take charge, it might as well be her.

So, with a deep sigh, she broke open the wax seal with her thumb, withdrew the pages from within, and held them under the light of Brent's cell phone. Then she began to read.

31

MAE

The party was over. The caterers and wedding staff were just finishing up their final tasks, and all the revelers had disappeared one by one. Eliza and Oliver had slunk off together, drunk and in love. Holly and Pete took the kids home after they found Alice curled up under a table, fast asleep. Debra and her date, Sheriff Mike, Lola, Marshall and the pretty young lady he'd brought (Lena something or other, a veterinarian)—each of them swept by to give Mae a kiss on the cheek and convey their best wishes to the mother of the happy couple, then went off into the night to settle into their own beds in their own homes.

Mae understood the sentiment, certainly. There was no place like home. But she was content to sit here for a while under the fairy lights. She soaked up the silence. After hours of chaos, it was actually quite nice to hear nothing at all aside from the normal sounds of a calm Nantucket evening. Waves, crickets, breeze in the treetops. Pure bliss.

She opened her eyes when she heard the gate to the cottage's backyard squeak open. Dominic rounded the corner, looking much the same as he had before—dapper, handsome, reserved, though he was on the far end of a handful of very strong whiskey drinks, so perhaps a little more flushed in the face than he might have been otherwise.

He came up to her with a kind of delicateness in his manner. Pulling up a chair, he set it down across from Mae and then sat down in it. He leaned back to look up into the night sky for a few long moments. Mae watched him and smiled. An unusual man, certainly. A lot went on in his mind that no one but him would ever be privy to. That was just the way things were, she supposed. There wasn't much that she could do about it other than ask to be let into his heart whenever he could find a way for her to do so.

Eventually, he brought his gaze from the sky back down to earth, then to Mae. "I owe you a great number of apologies," he said, with the air of someone who'd been thinking of what to say for a long time.

"Oh, Dominic, it's quite—"

He held up a hand to cut her off. "Please forgive me for interrupting. I believe I know you well enough by now to say that it is quite in your nature to be apologetic when the fault is all my own. I can see your frustration written in you, and I know that I am the one who is responsible." He sighed and scooted closer to her, taking one of her hands between his. "I came to you from a place of great sadness. In all the years since my daughter's passing, I chose to turn my face away from it. It wasn't until I came to you that I saw how grief ought to be handled. You are strong and wise, Mae. I hope you recognize that, because every person in your orbit sees it in you and draws strength and wisdom from your example."

Mae bit her lip. She wanted to cry. None of this felt real. Between the buzzing surge of the champagne she'd drunk, the ethereal glow of the fairy lights overhead, and Dominic's musical words, this felt like something out of a storybook, out of a dream. His hand was warm, though, and she could smell him—whiskey and books and cologne, all mingling together—and the beach just beyond the hedges, too, the brine and the sand and the gentle onrush of cool air as the storm edged closer to shore.

"I hope it is not a reach to tell you that I believe I love you, Mae Benson. To tell you that I believe that you helped me through something I did not know I needed help with. I hope I haven't brought an undue burden into your life."

"Dominic," she whispered. She cupped his face in her free hand. "You haven't brought any burdens anywhere, as far as I'm concerned. I only have simple words, not pretty words like yours, so I hope it's all right if I just tell you that I love you, too. I only want to know what's in your head and in your heart. That's all. If you tell me those things, then—well, then I think I'd be a very happy woman with you."

He smiled, slow and unsure at first but then gathering steam as her words settled into him. His eyes sparkled behind his glasses. She felt the rasp of his beard beneath her hand, lush and warm. He cleared his throat. "Then I suppose I ought to ask, just one more time to be sure: Is today the day you kick me out of the inn?"

Mae laughed. It was a callback to their old ritual, born on those quiet coffee mornings when she'd fallen in love with this man, little by little, like slipping into the ocean and finding that it's neither as cold nor as scary as you feared from your old vantage point way up on the shore.

"I don't think so," she replied. "Not tomorrow, either."

"That is certainly a relief," he said.

He kissed her, then, because there wasn't much else that either of them could say that mattered anymore. All the good words were taken. A kiss would have to do the rest.

Early that morning, before the wedding.

Mae had sat down at Dominic's writing nook in the early hours of the dawn, before Dominic was awake. Taking one of his treasured fountain pens, she put it to a piece of parchment paper and began to write. She didn't have a plan for what she was going to say, but as the pen found paper, the words flowed easily. She wrote what her heart said. And, though she'd never considered herself much of a writer, in the end, it came out just right.

~

"To my wonderful children,

First off, I ought to ask for your forgiveness. It would be better if I could tell you all these things in person. But every time I think about even starting to say what I'd like to say, I end up teary-eyed, and I plan on spending far too much time on my makeup for Eliza's wedding to ruin it like that. So a letter will have to do, I'm afraid.

I'd like to start by telling you a story. Your father built the house on Howard Street with his bare hands. It was a gift to me, or so he said. Secretly, I think he did it because he wanted to show off a little bit. That's all well and good—I liked seeing your father show off, and if he did it for my sake, well, so much the better.

In typical fashion, though, he couldn't bear to wait until he was done to reveal the secret to me. He was never much good at keeping secrets. He blindfolded me and drove me there, back in the days when we were staying in a cramped Nantucket bungalow far away from everything else. He sure took his time with the big reveal, too. Made me get out of the car and walk through the doorframe he hadn't yet built into the kitchen he hadn't yet finished. But I will remember for the rest of my days what he said when he finally let me take that blindfold off. He untied it from around my head and I blinked and blinked until I understood what was happening. Then he looked me in the eye and told me, "We are going to raise our family here."

Children, that is exactly what we did. You came quickly, one after the other, and each of you brought a new kind of joy into our lives. It was like learning that there were new colors being dreamt up, colors you'd never thought of before! Who knew there was an Eliza color? A Holly, a Sara, a Brent color?

But as much of a blessing as children are, it is a scary thing sometimes, being a parent. You have to learn to live with a kind of fear that gets hold of you and won't ever let go. I watched each of you sleep, I watched each of you cry, I watched each of you be sick and get hurt. And more often than not, I just had to sit and watch. There wasn't a darn thing I could do about it, at least not without doing you more harm than good in the process. Sometimes I had to tell you no. That is just as hard for a parent as it is for a child, you know. I want to give you the world, and that is not nearly as straightforward as it sounds.

Grow up you did, though, and as you did, you each inherited a richer and more beautiful world than anything I could've handed to you on a silver platter. That's not to say it was easy getting there. Though I think each of you is in such a gorgeous and happy place in your life right now, it wasn't always this way, nor will it stay this way forever. We had our bumps along the path, didn't we? And there are bumps yet to come. If I've learned anything in my time, it's that there are always bumps to come.

Now is the part where I must ask for your forgiveness a second time. I've never been much good with my words. I'm a straightforward woman at heart, I suppose. So if what I say next comes off as naive or cheesy, then do me the kindness of never telling me that. I mean these things sincerely, in my own way.

What gets us through the bumps is love. The beauty of that is that the world is full of as many kinds of love as there are people. You can love a dog, a man, a child, a beach, a moment, a cloud, a wave, a wedding, a word, a kiss, a fruit, a glass of wine, a shooting star. You can love your siblings and your mother and your father. You can love each of them in different and conflicting ways and that is okay, because if you hold that love truly in your heart than it can live there for as long as you let it, even if there is anger or grief or sadness there, too.

I have grief. I have sadness. Even anger, for your father being taken away from us far before I thought we would have to reckon with that possibility. What I'm learning (and yes, even an old dog like me can still learn a new trick or two) is that the things that hurt us are often the soil for the seeds of the love that is yet to come. I've said it before and I'll say it again: we are a forward-looking family, and that means we have to keep our eyes on the horizon. Let the hurt stay where it is. But when you wake up every day, choose to water love on top of that. It is what gets us through the nights. It is what keeps us together. It is what makes us whole.

Lastly, I ask for your forgiveness once more, because I've rambled for an awfully long time. This is supposed to be a night for celebrating, not for an old lady lecturing you on the meaning of life. I leave you with this: I love each of you with all my heart. For as long as I am here with you and forever afterwards, I will continue to love you. Promise me this, though: that you will love each other and that you will keep loving all those in your life who deserve such love. It is the best thing we can give to ourselves and to our fellow humans. At the end of the day, perhaps it is even the only thing.

With love forever,

Mom (and Dad)

Get Book 4 in the Sweet Island Inn series, NO LOVE LIKE NANTUCKET,
now!
Click here to start reading!

She built the Sweet Island Inn with her bare hands. But can Toni Benson build a life of happiness for herself?

Toni Benson's life has been a roller coaster.

Years ago, the heartbreak caused by a cheating ex-husband left her in tatters.

Then she discovered the run-down fixer-upper that would become the Sweet Island Inn.

For a while, things were good.

But when her brother Henry's tragic death sends her reeling all over again, she's back to square one.

So she sets off on an overseas journey, in hopes of learning from scratch what kind of woman she is meant to be.

She wasn't looking for love.

But it found her anyways.

Follow Toni's journey around the world as the Nantucket native navigates an explosive romance, an unbearable tragedy, and the prospect of starting life anew in her sixties.

In the end, only one thing is certain: there is no love like her love for Nantucket.

Travel back to the very beginnings of the Sweet Island Inn and follow along with the soaring highs and heartbreaking lows of Aunt Toni's story in NO LOVE LIKE NANTUCKET, the fourth installment of author Grace Palmer's beloved Sweet Island Inn series.

Click here to get swept away in NO LOVE LIKE NANTUCKET!

Or check out a sneak preview below:

Eighteen years earlier.
Atlanta, Georgia—June 15, 2000

Looking back on it, it would be easy for her to see that this was the kind of day that would change her life forever.

But at the time, it seemed to Toni Benson like it was just any other day. Just a normal Thursday in the middle of June, two weeks shy of her ninth wedding anniversary to her husband, Jared. The sun was shining; the birds were chirping; not a thing looked out of place.

Work that day went by in a flash. She spent most of it thinking about the surprise she was planning for her husband and browsing the Internet to double-check all the reservations she had made.

She'd never been much good at keeping secrets, especially not from Jared. He was the more mysterious of the two of them, certainly. As a matter of fact, in nine years of marriage and nearly twelve years of dating, she'd hardly learned much about him at all.

He always said, with the same sort of exasperated, '*Why are you even bothering with this?*' kind of tone, that there just wasn't much to know. He had a mother he didn't talk to and a hometown not worth mentioning. No father figure, no siblings, no past to speak of.

If she pressed him on it—when she'd had a glass of wine, say, or if she was just feeling a little nosy—he'd mention something vague about small town life. He'd been born in either Kansas or Arkansas— she never could remember which—and then, according to his version of events, he'd more or less shown up one day at the law firm where she worked as a paralegal. Fully formed, fully handsome, toting a charming smile and an impressive binder with which to pitch the firm's partners on his budding software company.

That was that, as far as origin stories go. He'd stayed behind after his presentation to flirt with her a bit, while she made excuses to linger and help him take down the backdrop he'd set up. Neither of them had been in any great hurry for him to leave.

Eventually, he'd asked to take her to dinner, and she'd pretended to ponder it for a bit before saying yes. He was awfully handsome, which made her a bit wary, but he seemed genuine enough. He had dimples set on either side of a country boy's *aw-shucks* kind of smile, and that felt like something that could be relied upon.

One date led to another, and before she knew it, they were moving in together in a little house in Virginia Highlands, an up-and-coming neighborhood near Atlanta.

It was fun for the longest time. Jared loved to take Toni on weekend drives in his little Mazda convertible around the rich neighborhoods in Cobb County. They'd slow down or stop outside the gates of the truly jaw-dropping mansions to ogle. He would whistle and slap Toni on the thigh to point out this ironwork fountain or that fluted marble column, which always made her laugh.

He was like a little kid on those excursions, just excited to see parts of the world that blew his hair back. And if he seemed a little overly keen on the trappings of the rich folks—well, who could blame him? They were awfully nice houses, after all. Anybody would get a little bit jealous, standing outside the gates of a home like that.

His excitement made her excited about life, too. He could be such an infectious, spontaneous guy, the kind of guy who shows up late to a dinner and immediately orders three bottles of wine for the table. Not because he was rich, though his software company had at long last begun to show some real promise in that department. But because it was simply a fun and spontaneous thing to do.

Which was why she was thrilled and nervous alike to be the one taking the lead in the "fun and spontaneous" category for their Fourth of July plans.

"You think he'll like this one, Solange?" she asked nervously. Her fellow paralegal, Solange—a gorgeous, slim woman with skin like caramel and perfect, voluminous ringlets that Toni, with her stick straight blonde hair, was eternally jealous of—looked over to Toni's computer screen for the umpteenth time that day.

"Stop," Solange counseled patiently. "You're freaking out. He's gonna love it. He loves you. You love him. What else matters?"

Toni bit her lip. "Everything matters, Sol. I want this to be fun. And you know Jared. He can be, I don't know... particular, sometimes."

That was true, too. For every memory of fun, life-of-the-party Jared she had, there was an equal and opposite memory of a time when he just hadn't at all reacted the way she thought he would to something.

The last time she'd tried to surprise him was at his thirty-fifth birthday party four years ago. She'd promised him a quiet, candlelit evening with just the two of them at a restaurant. But when they showed up to the dinner spot, his friends and coworkers came out of the woodworks to hoot and holler, "Surprise!"

She thought he'd laugh. She did so love his laugh.

He hadn't laughed, though. Not even a little bit. Instead, he'd stood stock-still in the middle of everyone for one impossibly long moment with his jaw and fists clenched before storming out of the restaurant steaming mad.

He wouldn't even look at her for a while after she followed him out into the night and tried to figure out what on earth was going on in his brain.

"I just don't like surprises," he growled again and again through gritted teeth, as if that explained anything whatsoever.

He seemed like he was terribly close to making her send everyone home. But at the last second, he'd relented and gone back inside. After reluctantly shaking everyone's hands and doing his rounds, he'd corralled a drink and nursed it by himself in the corner until it was time to go.

Toni didn't plan any surprises for a long, long while after that.

But for reasons she wasn't quite prepared to confront at the moment, it had begun to feel important to her over the last couple months to do something big and dramatic in her marriage.

She wished she knew why. If she'd had something she could point to, a specific instance or conversation or something along those lines, she might feel better about this plan she was conjuring up.

But, as frustrating as it was, she didn't have anything of the sort. All she had was a vague feeling that she ought to do *something*.

She'd tried to bring her concerns up to Solange or to her sister-in-law Mae or one of her other close friends at least half a dozen times since she'd first noticed the little thread of anxiety unspooling itself in the pit of her stomach. But every time she tried to muster up the words, she fell silent before she could spit it out. It just sounded silly, shrewish, insignificant.

Something's wrong in my marriage.

Like what? they would inevitably ask her. *Did he cheat? Did he lie? Did he hurt you?*

No, no, no, nothing of the sort. I can't say, exactly, can't quite put my finger on it. But I just know it's something.

If it sounded silly when she practiced that little exchange in her bathroom mirror, it would certainly sound silly in a conversation with one of her friends.

And if it sounded silly with one of her friends—well, then, Jared was likely to just roll his eyes and stomp out of the house rather than engage with it for even a fraction of a second.

He didn't have patience for anything that wasn't concrete, that he couldn't put his hands on. Toni had always found that funny, kind of ironic, that an artist like him was so insistent on material evidence. But, as with many other things, he didn't like when she pointed out that irony, so she made sure to steer well clear of it.

Still, the disquiet grew over time as she ignored it rather than shrinking. So after she'd decided that she had to do something, the question then became, what kind of something could she do?

And then one day, the solution had presented itself. They just needed some time to recharge and reconnect, she and Jared. A weekend away on Lake Lanier would be just the ticket. They could celebrate the Fourth of July, their ninth anniversary, and their blooming, everlasting love all at once. Three birds with one stone. Problems solved, presto change-o, cue the happily ever after.

It seemed like a neat answer to their unspecified problems. And besides, Jared had mentioned from time to time over the years that he wanted a boat. Toni figured that he'd get a kick out of renting one and captaining it out from the dock attached to their cabin. Truth be told, she quite liked the thought of a shirtless, suntanned Jared issuing nautical orders.

So she'd dove in headfirst to planning. When Toni Benson put her mind to something, she did it thoroughly. It was part of why she was so good at her job. Working in a law firm, especially with the high-powered, *"I want that document on my desk by yesterday!"* types who owned the practice that employed her, meant never missing a step.

She hadn't grown up wanting to be a paralegal. Mostly because not a single human being on earth grows up wanting to be a paralegal. But it suited her in its own stiff, paper-shuffling sort of way. There was a part of her soul that sang aloud when all the numbers in the spreadsheets tied out, or when she could clear the stacks of paper from her desk at the end of a satisfying work day and say, "Ahhh, all done."

She didn't need romance in her workplace. She had that at home. Or rather, she used to. And after she and Jared had their weekend away, wrapped up in each other, she'd have it back again in spades.

"Show me again, then, honey," Solange said. She was a wonderfully patient woman, thoughtful and kind, and Toni was glad to have her friendship now.

"You're the best," Toni murmured. She turned to her screen and started clicking through the photos one by one.

The cabin on the shore that she'd chosen really was gorgeous. The first picture showed a long wooden dock that reached out like a finger to stroke the surface of the lake. The water around it was still, smooth, and so blue that it made her eyes hurt. She was already savoring the thought of unwinding out there in the evening, sipping a glass of wine as the sun set over the trees in the distance.

The rest of the house was just as cute. It was one of those homes built to coax its residents out onto the wraparound porch whenever possible. Half of the porch was screened in and festooned with fans to keep beating at the lazy summer air while someone snoozed in the hammock or one of the big, cozy rocking chairs. The other part was open to the breeze. Tasteful red cloth upholstery tied together all of the patio furniture.

Indoors was rustic and snug. Blond wooden beams held up the ceiling, the stairs, the mantlepiece, and the railings that lined the walkways between upstairs bedrooms. She loved how the light of the homey, DIY mason jar lamps in the kitchen added a warm shimmer to the wooden cabinetry.

And the master bedroom upstairs, with its massive French double doors, opened right up onto a second intimate porch holding another pair of rocking chairs that practically had "Jared" and "Toni" written on them already.

"If he doesn't like that, then you're gonna have to throw the whole man out," Solange said wryly.

Toni laughed, maybe a little louder than she intended to. She glimpsed Rogelio, one of the sterner partners, glance up in irritation from his corner office.

"Just tell me one more time that he'll love it."

"Honey," Solange said, resting a comforting hand on Toni's forearm. "He's going to love it. Just ease up. Have a fun weekend. Drink some wine, smooch your hubby, watch the sunset. You're gonna have fun, okay, doll?"

When she said it like that, there was no room for disagreement. Toni smiled. This time, she meant it.

A little while later, it was finally quitting time, thank the Lord. Toni swept her things into her bag, turned off her computer, and spent a minute making sure that everything was neatly organized so she could start tomorrow with a clean slate.

She was just about to turn and head for her car in the parking lot when Rogelio strode up to her desk and announced his arrival with a rap of his knuckles.

"Hi, Rog," Toni said with a smile. "You need anything from me? I was just about to head out."

Rogelio was a tall, tanned man from the Philippines with a shiny bald spot and big hands that were constantly in motion. He had a way of talking, sort of stern and borderline angry, that some of the other paralegals found intimidating or condescending. But his mannerisms had never bothered Toni. He just liked work to be done right, and she liked doing it right. In fact, they got along fairly well.

"Did you get the deposition transcripts from the Martinelli trial finished?"

"The coroner's or the husband's?" she asked immediately.

"Husband's."

She nodded. "In your inbox already. The coroner's, too, actually," she added with a wink.

"Did you set up the admin hearing for the Gantt Co. case?"

"July 17th, 4 p.m."

"Did you—"

"Dr. Tompkins from Georgia Tech will be providing expert testimony on the blood spatters, the latest draft of the motion for retrial is uploaded to the firm's cloud, and I sent the appendices for the two memos in the Buchanan thing over to Desiree to approve."

Rogelio, for a change, was actually smiling by the time Toni was done listing off rapid-fire all the tasks that she'd already squared away.

"You know, sometimes I don't know why I even bother to ask. You are always on top of things. What would we do without you, Toni?" he mused playfully.

She laughed. "You'd find a way."

"I'm not so sure we would."

"Need anything else from me before I head out?"

"No, no," he said, waving a hand in a fatherly sort of way at her. "Go home. Tell Jared I said hello."

"Will do. Have a good night, Rogelio. G'night, Solange!"

She waved goodbye to everyone as she looped her purse over her shoulder and strode out into the early evening sun.

Atlanta traffic being what it was, the drive home was agonizingly long. But that was all right with Toni. She usually did her best thinking on her commute to and from work. Something about the warm silence of the car and the sun rising or setting over the downtown skyscrapers always kept the wheels in her head turning nicely.

She spent the first fifteen minutes going over and over the plan for the lakehouse. They would get there on Sunday, two days before the Fourth, so they could unpack, unwind, and make a quick run to the grocery store to pick up food and wine for the remainder of their vacation.

She had a menu planned already—seared scallops with endive and radicchio, which would pair perfectly with the buttery, oaky chardonnay she had in mind—and was smiling at the thought of strolling down the dock after dinner, hand in hand with Jared, to watch the boaters heading home in the dying evening light.

Just then, her cell phone started to buzz in her purse. She fished it out and smiled even bigger when she saw who was calling.

"Mae, dear!" she cooed. "How are you?"

"Up to my eyeballs in stuff to do, as always," Mae replied, though Toni could hear the hint of a smile on the edge of her voice.

"You wouldn't have it any other way," Toni said with a laugh.

"No, of course not. But I reserve the right to complain."

"Hey," Toni said, "you're the one who chose to marry my brother. I could've told you that he wouldn't exactly be fumbling all over himself to help you with the household stuff."

Mae laughed at that. "Oh God, no, I don't let him anywhere near the chores. Last time I told him to do the dishes, he scrubbed all the finish off my best cast iron skillet. I darn near made him sleep in the doghouse for the night."

"Head in the clouds, that one," Toni agreed. "You guys good?"

"We're fabulous, hon, of course."

"How're the kids?"

"Let's see. Give me one sec, I just have to remember their names..."

Toni chuckled. "How you manage four of them is beyond me. Especially a little terror on wheels like your youngest."

"Brent is a devil with an angel's smile," Mae agreed. "It amazes me to this day how quick he took to running. He crawled for all of three steps before he decided it wasn't fast enough for him. Come to think of it, Sara was much the same."

"The two of them have a lot of fire. It's a good thing your older ones balance them out a bit."

"That they do," Mae said. "Although that's hard in its own way. Eliza is fourteen, and she is certainly proving that everything folks say about teenage girls is true."

Toni furrowed her brow. "Have you two been butting heads?"

"No, not quite. She's so... inwardly focused, I suppose. Does very well at school, so it's not that. Does well at everything, actually. But she keeps things quite close to the chest. I just worry about her, is all."

"That's your job, hon. But Eliza is a smart cookie. She'll be just fine. I have no doubt about that."

"Of course, of course."

"And Holly?"

"Sweet as molasses. Loves her momma, loves her daddy, loves her siblings, loves her life."

Toni grinned. "Truer words have never been spoken. That one is heaven-sent." She could hear the clink and clatter of plates in the background. Mae must be preparing dinner for the family. "What're you serving up tonight?"

"I'm tired, so I took the easy way out and made meatloaf," Mae said absent-mindedly.

Toni rolled her eyes. "I know darn well what that means, Mae. You aren't fooling anyone. You've probably been in the kitchen all afternoon sculpting a meatloaf made by the angels."

"Shush," Mae scolded playfully, "you don't know that."

"Somehow, I think I hit the nail on the head."

"Well, anyways," said Mae with a laugh, changing the subject, "the reason I was calling in the first place was because Henry told me you had news about the Fourth. Are you and Jared still coming up?"

"Oh!" Toni exclaimed, feeling suddenly guilty. "That blockhead didn't fill you in? Lord, I could bop him sometimes. I'm so sorry for the last minute change, Mae, but Jared and I are going to get a little cabin up by Lake Lanier for the weekend instead of coming home to Nantucket."

"That's a bummer!" Mae said sadly. "We're going to miss the two of you here. The fireworks show is not the same without Aunt Toni and Uncle Jared around."

"I know, I know. But I think—I think we need this."

Mae must've picked up on the shift in Toni's tone, because all she said was a soft, "Oh?"

"Yeah," Toni said, gnawing at her lip again, just like she'd been doing all day. The traffic in front of her had hardly budged since she'd gotten on the phone with Mae. Suddenly, she felt uncomfortable in the car, like she wanted to get out right this instant. Gone were the happy vibes she'd felt upon leaving the office, the certainty that this lakehouse plan was the remedy for the niggling doubts she had done her best to ignore for months now. In their place, she just felt clammy and itchy and impatient.

"Is everything okay with the two of you?" Mae asked carefully.

Toni thought about unloading the blabbing stream-of-consciousness anxieties she'd kept bottled up for so long. It still wouldn't make any sense, and there was no telling if it would make her feel any better. But she felt the urge to do so nonetheless.

The problem was that Mae just wouldn't understand. That wasn't her fault—it was just that she and Toni's brother, Henry, were so head-over-heels in love with each other that there wasn't even the slightest bit of room for doubts to creep in.

It would be wrong of Toni to be mad or jealous about that. It was such a sweet thing that a love like theirs could exist in this world. Whenever she saw the two of them holding hands under the dinner table or glanced at a family picture and saw Henry's protective arm draped over Mae's shoulders, her heart softened a little bit.

But it always hardened up again right after. Because, as much as she wanted that from Jared, it wasn't forthcoming.

Yet.

Maybe things were going to change. Maybe, like a good wine, her marriage just needed some time to mature into something delicate and beautiful like what Henry and Mae had.

The story sounded convincing enough that she decided not to answer Mae's question honestly. So, instead of opening up, she blew a stray hair back from her forehead and said with a laugh in her voice, "Oh, we're lovely. Better than ever, actually. Jared just got hired for a big project that starts the week of the holiday, though, so we couldn't find a way to make the travel work. This was the next best thing."

"Oh, well, that's fabulous then!" Mae said cheerily.

"Yeah, yeah," Toni said, still clinging to the bravado she'd mustered up. "Anyways, sorry to cut you off, but traffic is a bear right now, so I should probably focus on driving."

"Of course. Love you, Toni. Talk soon. And if we don't speak before then, have a lovely trip to the lake!"

"Love you, too, Mae. Tell my oaf of a brother and your sweet little kids I said hello."

"Will do. Buh-bye."

They hung up and Toni let the phone fall in her lap. Part of her was sad that they wouldn't be going to Nantucket. There was no place quite like her home. But after the phone call with Mae, she suddenly wasn't sure that going there would be a good idea either.

Mae loved her husband and loved her kids and they all loved her. They had a happy home, a full home.

And that, more than anything, was what Toni was missing.

She and Jared had chatted about having children on and off through the years, though it had never led anywhere. Jared hadn't ever said it outright, but Toni got the feeling that he had no intention of raising a family. At least, no intention of raising a family *with her.*

Perhaps it wasn't fair to him to add that last part, since he'd given no indication that it was something wrong with Toni in particular that stood in the way of their having kids together. But she just had a feeling. And, like the feelings of doubt creeping into her relationship, they wouldn't go away, no matter how hard she tried to ignore them.

The lake would fix things. She looked in the rearview mirror and said it out loud, as if to test the truth of it. "The lake will fix things."

Say it again, she whispered internally. *One more time, with feeling.*

"The lake will fix things."

She wanted so badly to believe it. But in the musty silence of the car, it didn't sound convincing at all.

Click here to keep reading NO LOVE LIKE NANTUCKET!

A NOTE FROM THE AUTHOR

Thanks so much for reading! I sincerely hope you enjoyed the third installment in the Sweet Island Inn series, *No Wedding Like Nantucket*.

I just wanted to take a moment to thank each and every one of you who has read my books, shared them with your loved ones, and written to let me know that my work touched you in some way.

It means the world to me to know that my words are making a difference in the life of even one person out there. So, from the bottom of my heart—thank you, thank you, thank you. I can't wait to keep going. There is lots more to come.

With love,

Grace Palmer

JOIN MY MAILING LIST!

Click the link below to join my mailing list and receive updates, freebies, release announcements, and more!

JOIN HERE:

https://readerlinks.com/l/1060002

ALSO BY GRACE PALMER

Sweet Island Inn

No Home Like Nantucket (Book 1)

No Beach Like Nantucket (Book 2)

No Wedding Like Nantucket (Book 3)

No Love Like Nantucket (Book 4)

Willow Beach Inn

Just South of Paradise (Book 1)

Just South of Perfect (Book 2)

Just South of Sunrise (Book 3)

Made in the USA
Monee, IL
18 February 2021

60862047R00144